I JUST WANNA BE A GIRL

A COLLECTION OF BLOGPOSTS

LEKHAA MEENAKSHISUNDARAM

This book is dedicated to every single person who inspired me.

Contents

Contents

Contents

Contents

Contents

Acknowledgements

My first thanks would obviously go to my big brother and best friend, Anderlin. He is the inspiration - whether directly or indirectly - for so many of my entries. He has been reading my blogs from the very first day I started writing and has been my constant supporter throughout my journey. He took the time to comment on each of my entries objectively. A lot of my entries are based on my experiences with him, things I have said to him, or that he has said to me.

Then, my thanks to Sharan, for being another one of my sources of inspiration, and for allowing me to use his name. Thanks to Shane, Harish, Christopher, and Mugunthan for letting me use your names. I have to extend my gratitude to Deepak Anna, who I met very briefly, yet was a source of inspiration to me - for my writing and otherwise.

My thanks to Veena for looking through every single one of my entries and making sure that they were flawless. Thank you to Kavin and Swetha for reading my entries consistently.

Next, I have to extend my gratitude to my professor Dr. Samuel Rufus for posing the challenge that led to this book.

My thanks to the creators of The Vampire Diaries for providing vibrant characters for my analyses. My thanks to Stephenie Meyer, for her magnificent Twilight Saga. Thank you to all my favourite childhood authors for fueling my love for writing.

This book would be impossible without Taylor Swift. A chunk of my entries are based on the lyrics of her songs, or the titles of the songs themselves.

My immense gratitude to everyone reading this book. Thank you for taking the time to read what I have to say.

Author's Note

Dear reader,

The story of how this book came to be is pretty unique. One day, my professor, Dr. Samuel Rufus came into my class and announced a blogging challenge. He told us that he wanted us to be consistent bloggers. He also provided us with an incentive. He promised us a cash prize for 30 days and for 60 days, he assured us that he would help us publish our entries into a book. I had always aspired to be a writer and I instantly accepted the challenge. The book you are about to read is a result of that challenge.

This book is a collection of carefully selected and compiled entries that I wrote over the course of 150 days. It ranges through topics like womanhood, The Vampire Diaries, Taylor Swift, my brother, my friends, some of my philosophical thoughts, and much more. There are a lot of general entries as well.

The title of this book is interesting as well. I came up with the title during a time when I felt depraved of and craved female company. I had been spending all my time with guys. While this is normal for me - and I am totally okay with it, I felt the need to talk to a girl. I just wanted some time to gossip and moan about random things. I just wanted to be a girl.

I hope you enjoy reading my thoughts. (You can find what other people think about my thoughts at the end of the book. I have put in some of my favourite comments.)

With loads of love,
Lekhaa

CHAPTER ONE

REMEMBER THAT YOU ARE A WOMAN

Yes, I am one of those girls who spends most of her time with guys. That doesn't mean I don't need to remember the fact that I am a woman. Until recently, I thought I would be totally fine with spending all my time with a group of boys. At one point, I found myself deprived of all the things that made me a woman. I didn't feel respected as a woman. Even though I had a group of male friends around me, I felt an extreme need for female companionship. There are just some things you need another girl for, right?

I needed a girl to gossip to. I needed to moan and whine and just talk about the guys in my life. It might sound shallow, but I think it is one of the basic needs of a woman. When I was reading "Men Are from Mars, Women Are from Venus" by John Gray, I noticed how he claimed that women need to be listened to to be validated. That obviously means having someone to talk to. What better place to go to than another woman who makes you feel validated? The world needs more women who motivate other women when they are in need.

I don't mean to say that men aren't good listeners. In my experience, men can also be patient and listen to what you have to say. But, like I said earlier, sometimes you just need a girl. You need a female perspective. Some quality 'girl time' can make all the difference. It doesn't need to be long and it doesn't need to be planned out. Just being in the presence of other strong women can feel empowering.

Remember to embrace your femininity!

CHAPTER TWO

WHY DOES A GIRL NEED A BROTHER IN HER LIFE?

I grew up without an attentive brother figure (or rather, they didn't really know I was around), but I have always longed for a big brother. I've always been on the lookout for people I could consider a big brother but was unsuccessful until recently. I always idolized my big brothers, even though they never really acknowledged my existence. A lot of my habits and preferences are based on theirs.

First and foremost, a big brother is someone whose example you can follow. You can learn a lot from them. They teach you how to look at things and provide a unique perspective. They know you inside out and know how to reassure you appropriately. He shows you that he is your number one supporter and biggest fan. They are a reliable source of information.

A big brother shows you what unconditional love is. Yes, it's his job to chastise you, but beyond that, you can believe that it's because he loves you so much that he is strict sometimes. You know that he's not going to disown you or love you any less just because you messed up. He's going to help you out of your mess and teach you to do better next time.

On a less serious note, a brother is your ticket into the world of sports. He's also the one who's going to let you crash his car or bike when you're learning how to drive. He's going to put his own life on the line while teaching you how to drive. He toughens you up every time you listen to him teasing you. He teaches you about other men, how they think, and how to carry yourself around them. On the whole, you really can't live without your big brother.

I always felt like I didn't have anyone to look out for me, anyone to tell me what's right and what's not, or anyone who loved me unconditionally. I had nowhere to turn when I felt alone in the world. There were times when all I wanted was for one of my brothers to talk to me or even just be around (which didn't happen).

I now have the privilege of having the perfect brother figure. I feel comfortable taking the time and space to figure myself out, knowing that he has my back. The trust I place in him is astronomical and unequivocal. He goes out of his way to make sure I know that he loves me. He reminds me that I'm not really alone in the world anymore. He's always the first person I want to talk to about my achievements and his approval means the world to me. He's my greatest supporter and my backbone.

He is undoubtedly one of the best people I've had the privilege of meeting and I'm extremely grateful for him.

Remember to tell your brother that you love and cherish him.

Why Does A Woman Need A Male Best Friend?

Most of my best friends are guys. I have always felt like there is less competition and judgment in a male-female friendship. Most friendships between girls have some level of competition between them, whether it's over something as trivial as looks or something bigger. Some women pretend like they care, but deep down, they just want to get ahead of you. On the other hand, I have found friendships between men and women to be pure.

A male best friend is someone who would be the first person to give you practical solutions to your problems. He will tell you what's right and what's wrong. He might sound harsh and you might think that he doesn't care about you whereas in reality, he cares deeply and wants to make sure you know what you're doing.

Male friends aren't going to be jealous of you if you succeed. They genuinely revel in your success and comfort you through your failures. They also are really good secret keepers and can comfort you when you need it. They can help you put things into perspective and make sure you're thinking clearly. Your male best friend will always be protective over you and unconditionally supportive. He would never let you make bad decisions about the other men in your life, unlike some of your female friends who would give you insincere advice because they are secretly jealous of you.

On a less serious note, sharing your secrets with male best friends is recommended because they don't listen to half of what you say. They don't understand another part and they forget the rest. (Sorry, I couldn't help quoting an Instagram reel here). In all seriousness, men are really good secret keepers.

Male friendships have considerably less drama compared to female ones. When you're with your male friends, you can just let yourself go. You can be free without worrying about being judged about something that you say or do. You deserve the respite from the drama. Take it!

CHAPTER FOUR

The Popularity Of Love Triangles In Literature And Media

Why are there so many love triangles in books or series? I mean, I can think of a bunch right off the top of my head. There's the classic Edward-Bella-Jacob from Twilight, Stefan-Damon-Elena from The Vampire Diaries, Klaus-Caroline-Tyler from The Vampire Diaries, Jackson-Hayley-Elijah from The Originals, Harry-Cho-Cedric from Harry Potter, Ron-Hermione-Krum from Harry Potter, Peeta-Katniss-Gale from the Hunger Games. I'm sure there are a hundred more that I haven't mentioned.

Recently, I stopped to think about why authors and creators try to include love triangles in their work. I realized that love triangles create tension. It keeps readers invested in the story. It also makes readers ship characters together, to the extent that they create entire fandoms for the characters, like the well-known Stelena and Delena ships.

Love triangles allow writers to delve into character development. We get to see all sides of the characters. We get to watch as the character in the middle falls for both of the others, one at a time, and then watch as he or she chooses one in the end. There's also the off chance that he or she leaves both of them, deciding to be with someone else or deciding that it's better to be alone. We as the audience get to watch what the character is going to do. We can't predict the outcome of the situation. When the story is in the first person perspective, you get to feel like you're loved by not just one but two people, vying for your attention. It makes you want to keep reading or watching.

CHAPTER FIVE

THE DIFFERENT PERCEPTIONS OF VAMPIRES

Vampire lore has become a huge part of the literary world. The first mention of vampires in literature was in the epic poem 'Thalaba the Destroyer' by Robert Southey. The most iconic and well-known vampire is undoubtedly Dracula, created by Bram Stoker. Dracula was the most definitive definition of the vampire in fiction until he wasn't anymore. In 2005, Stephanie Meyer took the world by storm with her magnificent Twilight.

Dracula is portrayed as a tall, thin, white-haired man with a mustache. He has sharp fingernails, pointy ears, and long, sharp teeth. He has superhuman strength and doesn't cast a shadow or a reflection in the mirror. He is nearly indestructible (compared to humans), can defy gravity to a certain extent, and possesses superhuman agility. Dracula has powerful hypnotic and telepathic abilities. He can manipulate the weather and can control other animals. He can even change his form. Above all, he is immortal.

Dracula can turn humans into vampires by biting them. He doesn't require anything but human blood to sustain him. The sun isn't fatal to him but weakens him considerably. He is doomed to a state of death-sleep during the day. He sleeps open-eyed, unable to move.

In comparison, vampires in the Twilight Saga aren't affected by the sun in the same way Dracula is. They are said to sparkle in the sun, risking their exposure. They are portrayed as pale-skinned and they have eyes that change colour depending on how recently they have fed. Meyer twists the traditional tale with her idea that vampires can survive on animal blood. They can only be killed if they are dismembered and burned. They have special powers and perfect features, making them physically attractive to their prey, i.e., humans. Vampires in Twilight can turn humans into vampires through the venom in their bite, similar to Dracula. They also have superhuman strength, speed, and agility.

These are only 2 of the countless perceptions of vampires in recent times. There will undoubtedly be many more twists on the traditional tale of the vampire which I, for one, am looking forward to.

CHAPTER SIX

EDWARD THE MASOCHIST AND BELLA THE ADRENALINE JUNKIE

Stephanie Meyer released a new book titled Midnight Sun a couple of years ago. When I first read it, I didn't really analyze it much. It was just magical to read Twilight (which is one of my favourite books) from Edward's point of view. I loved looking into Edward's mind and witnessing how much he loved Bella.

When I was rereading it a few days ago, I realized how masochistic Edward really is. He accepts that he is in the story, but I never really got it until now. For those of you who aren't familiar with the story, Edward is a vampire who sustains himself on animal blood. Bella's blood is like a drug to him. (His own words.) It's nearly impossible for Edward to resist the allure of her blood. It brings him physical pain to be in her presence. It's like inhaling fire to him. Yet, he puts himself through that torture. Yes, you could say that it's all for love that he does this. I agree with that too. But, in the end, subjecting himself to that pain is masochistic.

Another aspect to consider is what would happen if Edward accidentally lost control when he was around Bella. He wouldn't be able to stop himself once he tasted her blood. That would also cause him unendurable pain. Isn't it masochistic to test his control like that, with her life on the line? How would he fare if something was to happen to her? He admits throughout the story that her life meant more to him than hers. He says that she is his lifeline and that she is a permanent change in his life.

Then, let's look at Bella. She could be considered an adrenaline junkie – the way she flirts with death. She knows that Edward could kill her in seconds, yet, she does nothing to distance herself from him. She refuses to let him go. She seems to enjoy living on the edge like that. You could look at this as the amount of trust that she places in Edward. You could say that she has complete faith in his love for her and knows that it would destroy him to hurt her. But, you could also look at her as someone who takes risks.

I'm sure some of you might not agree with the way I portrayed Edward and Bella here. Let me get one thing straight. I still love the story. I still love the two of them as characters and as individuals. This was just something that struck me.

DAMON SALVATORE: HERO OR VILLAIN

Well, that is certainly one of the most controversial questions. Damon Salvatore is one of the 3 main characters in the show, The Vampire Diaries. He is shown in contrast to his brother Stefan Salvatore. In the first half of the first season, Damon is portrayed as the villain, but with his looks and style, people couldn't help but fall for him.

When Damon is first introduced, it's clear that Stefan is the good brother while Damon is the bad one. The audience can't help but be captivated by him, but it's impossible to excuse his villainous deeds. It's also clear that everything he does, he does in the name of love. His love for Katherine is undeniable.

Damon Salvatore has a complex personality, complete with many admirable traits and serious flaws as well. He is charismatic, loyal, protective, and humorous. On the other hand, Damon is extremely impulsive, selfish, violent, manipulative and volatile. Most of the time, Damon can't figure out whether he wants to be the hero or the villain. In the first couple of seasons, he has a lot of trouble trying to 'be good' for Elena. He had one of the greatest character arcs and turned out to be one of the greatest heroes of the show.

Damon was constantly being compared to his brother, even during his human life. It started with his father, followed by Katherine and then Elena. This led him to develop an inferiority complex. His actions sometimes go against his interests. His disregard for Bonnie and Jeremy led to Elena hating and alienating him, which he hated and had to work hard to fix. He has a good heart and was always willing to put his life on the line for the (few) people he loved. He is a great friend who'll do anything for them even to the extent of endangering himself. He proves this after he makes peace with Bonnie and Caroline. He becomes an amazing brother and friend.

I am a complete Damon fan girl and unshakably believe he is a hero.

CHAPTER EIGHT

KATHERINE PIERCE, THE QUEEN OF HELL

Katherine Pierce or Katerina Petrova, no matter how you refer to her, is the worst - or best, whichever way you look at it - villain in TVD history. However, it's hard not to look at her as a victim of circumstance.

Katherine is described as manipulative and ruthless. She will stop at nothing to get what she wants. She has a strong sense of self-preservation and will always, ALWAYS, put herself first.

Everyone always claims that she ruined their lives while glazing over everything that happened to her. She was chased out of her own family home. Her family considered that she was a disgrace after she gave birth to a daughter. Her newborn daughter was ripped from her arms moments after she gave birth. She was coveted for her blood and the abilities it possessed. She was forced to kill herself to save her life. Her family was mercilessly slaughtered. She became a vampire and then was pursued for centuries.

She was on the run for the entirety of her vampire life. In between all this, she turned the Salvatore brothers into vampires which, everyone claims, ruined their lives.

Let's think for a moment, shall we? If Katherine hadn't turned them, would the brothers have met their true loves, Elena and Caroline? Would they have found peace? Yes, Katherine was evil. She did a lot of despicable things. She is impulsive and longs for luxury. But, next time you judge her, remember what she has been through.

Yes, Katherine is the literal 'Queen of Hell' but she had her reasons for being evil. Not that anything justifies her malevolent deeds, of course.

Remember, she was a survivor.

CHAPTER NINE

CAROLINE FORBES: A CHARACTER ANALYSIS

Caroline Forbes is one of the main characters on the show, 'The Vampire Diaries.' Apart from the three central characters, she has the most screen time.

In the first season, Caroline was introduced as a stereotypical blond girl. She was one of the popular girls at school and was the captain of the cheerleading squad. She was also pretty headstrong and competitive. She had a high degree of leadership and was always the one organizing things. She was the daughter of the town's sheriff and possessed a high social prestige. Underneath her loving nature and confident exterior, Caroline is very insecure, neurotic, and a control freak. There were a lot of flaws and complexities in her character, which she eventually overcame, leading to her immense character development.

Caroline became a vampire, which led to a drastic change in her personality. This showed her the world in a new light. She outgrew her insecurities and became more responsible and caring. Being a vampire was what made her truly alive. As a new vampire, she had uncanny control over herself.

Caroline grew a lot over the years. She started dating Damon because she was jealous of Elena's relationship with Stefan. She finally ended up falling in love with her best friend and vampire mentor, Stefan Salvatore. She was a mother to two surrogate daughters. She also turned Klaus Mikaelson, the worst evil to befall Mystic Falls, into someone good. She saw the best in people and believed that anyone could be redeemed.

I believe that Caroline was the character who showed the most character development throughout the season. People usually dismiss her after watching a couple of episodes. I think that they should give her a chance. They should watch her grow and become comfortable with who she is.

CHAPTER TEN

DOES ELENA PLAY THE VICTIM CARD TOO MUCH?

Elena Gilbert is the female lead in the CW's 'The Vampire Diaries.' She is introduced to us with her tragic past. She just lost her parents in a car accident that she was in but somehow survived. Elena went on to learn that she was adopted. She met her birth parents and lost them soon. She also lost her guardian and friend. She lost her brother, which led to her turning off her humanity (which vampires can do.) She also lost her best friend followed by her soul mate.

Elena went through so much and was undoubtedly a victim. However, the other characters on the show have faced equal grief. Yet, Elena is the one who's always crying or holding in her tears. People are always taking care of her and making sure that she doesn't break. Her friends have died and come back to life. They have lost as many people as Elena has, friends, siblings, and parents.

In my opinion, people should stop giving her so much attention. She has faced a lot, but she should be able to face it like an adult. I feel like she seeks attention too much every time she talks about her dead loved ones.

If you take away her grief, there's not a lot of her character left. I think that's why the show's writers kept coming back to that.

CHAPTER ELEVEN

WHY IS TAYLOR SWIFT SO IMPORTANT?

"Taylor Swift is actually for the girls who were known but never popular, who fit in with many friend groups but never in the group chats, talked to at school but never invited to parties, for the girls who have friends but still feel lonely because they were never their best friend's favourite."

Yes, I am one of those girls. I read this on an Instagram reel and it got me thinking. I felt like I really understood what the creator was trying to say and when I looked at the comments, I could tell that there were a lot of girls who felt the same way.

Taylor is amazing, I would vouch for this anywhere. When you listen to her songs, she transports you to her world where you can forget everything that you're worrying about. In "Back to December," she takes you to heartbreak and the best part is, when you're listening to her music, it acts as an outlet. In "Love Story," she makes you feel like you're Juliet herself, waiting for a prince to sweep you off your feet. In "You Belong with Me", she makes you feel like you are the girl on the bleachers, crushing on someone who only looks at you as a friend and is way out of your league. Her songs are really relatable.

Taylor's songs don't let you feel lonely. When you're listening to her music, she makes you feel like she's singing to you and to you alone. She makes you feel like you are HER favourite. She doesn't make you feel like you're out of her league.

CHAPTER TWELVE

Taylor Swift's 'You Belong With Me'

Taylor Swift's 'You Belong With Me' is undoubtedly one of the crowd's favourite songs. If you look closely, there is a really deep meaning contained in her artistic lyrics. It speaks of unrequited teenage love and tells a story in less than 4 minutes.

Taylor – or the speaker – starts by explaining how she overheard her best friend, whom she had a crush on, fighting with his girlfriend. She says how his girlfriend doesn't understand her friend, unlike her. She believes that she knows her friend better than anyone else.

Taylor shows us how this 'other' girl is a popular cheerleader, a stereotypical 'girly girl' and she is pretty much her polar opposite. She is the stereotypical 'girl next door.' She pictures herself sitting on the bleachers, waiting for the moment when her friend realizes that he has a perfect girl – the speaker – waiting for him.

The speaker imagines how her life would be if he was hers as she believed. She notices that her friend is upset even though he claims that he is okay. She thinks it's because of this girl that he is upset. She goes on to chastise him for being with a girl who makes him unhappy. She remembers all the good memories she had with her friend. She claims that she knows him better than anyone on the planet.

Taylor really connects with the audience with the story she tells. We can all relate to the speaker. I'm sure we have all had a moment when we felt like we knew our friends better than their significant other. 'You Belong With Me' is a song dedicated to all those friends who've waited in the wings for their friend to notice that they have feelings for each other. They have to watch their friend love someone who is clearly wrong for them.

CHAPTER THIRTEEN

'Stay Stay Stay' An Analysis

Taylor Swift's 'Stay, Stay, Stay' is not considered one of her best works, but I disagree. There is a magical way the upbeat music is at odds with the intense lyrics. She starts her song with the way she fought with her boyfriend. She goes on to ask him to come back so they can talk their problems out. She is shocked when he comes back to her (wearing a football helmet) and agrees to talk to her.

In the chorus, Taylor asks him to stay. The way the lyrics have been written shows us how much she values the relationship or rather, loves the idea of being in love. The line "You think that it's funny when I'm mad, mad, mad," shows us that there are problems in the relationship but that Taylor doesn't acknowledge them. She is in denial. She thinks it's best if they both stay together.

> "Before you, I'd only dated self-indulgent takers
> Who took all of their problems out on me
> But you carry my groceries and now I'm always laughing

> *I love you because you have given me no choice*
> *but to..."*

These lines show all the good parts of the relationship. She says that he is the best partner she has had. She talks about how he is different from the men in her past. She says that she is genuinely happy with him and goes on to plead with him in the following chorus.

> *"You took the time to memorize me*
> *My fears, my hopes and dreams*
> *I just like hanging out with you*
> *All the time*
> *All those times that you didn't leave*
> *It's been occurring to me*
> *I'd like to hang out with you*
> *For my whole life"*

This bridge is unequivocally the most romantic part of the song. She's convincing herself and the audience that this man really loved her. She reminds herself that he took the time to get to know her as a person and genuinely cared about her. She states that the fact that he didn't leave when things got tough made her realize that she really liked this man and wanted to be with him forever.

She shows a bit of fear before her last chorus when she says "No one else is gonna love me when I get mad, mad, mad."

This song is basically a plea for her lover to stay with her. She says that no one could ever love her like he did. The lyrics hurt when you really look at them and feel them.

CHAPTER FOURTEEN

WHAT IS 'BACK TO DECEMBER' TRYING TO TELL US?

Back to December is first and foremost an apology from Taylor Swift to her ex-boyfriend. Taylor tells us how she fell in love with him. She tells us how they were good friends in the summer and how she realized she loved him in the fall. She says that she started having doubts when winter came. This leads to her rebuffing his love when he confesses to her. She uses the change in the seasons to show how their love progressed.

At the beginning of the song, it looks like she's meeting her ex after their break-up. She remembers that the last time they met, he gave her roses and she left them there to die, symbolizing how she broke his heart. She sings about how she swallows her pride and sets aside her ego as she apologizes to him. She tells him that she has done nothing but miss him and wishes she realized what she had when they were together.

She said that she couldn't sleep because of how much she missed him. She kept replaying their break-up in her mind. She regrets not calling him on his birthday. This is where she inserts the story of how she fell in love with him.

> "*I miss your tan skin, your sweet smile*
> *So good to me, so right*
> *And how you held me in your arms that September night*
> *The first time you saw me cry*
> *Maybe this is wishful thinking*
> *Probably mindless dreamin'*
> *But if we loved again, I swear I'd love you right*
> *I'd go back in time and change it, but I can't*
> *So if the chain is on your door, I understand*"

This bridge is where the apology becomes a plea. Taylor wants to go back to the relationship. She realizes that this probably won't happen. She talks about how she wants to rewind time and fix her mistakes, but she knows it's impossible. She understands that he is hurt, but still hopes he will take her back.

Back to December is one of my favourite Taylor Swift songs and the bridge makes me cry every time I listen to it. Taylor's voice has the power to put you in her shoes. You can feel the heartbreak she was going through.

CHAPTER FIFTEEN

'SPEAK NOW' SAID TAYLOR

Speak Now is one of my favourite Taylor Swift songs.

"I am not the kind of girl
Who should be rudely barging in
On a white veil occasion
But you are not the kind of boy
Who should be marrying the wrong girl"

Taylor pictures herself as a girl who has to watch her true love marry the wrong girl - basically a girl who isn't her. She paints this other woman as 'evil' when she says things like "and she is yelling at a bridesmaid, somewhere back inside her room, wearing a gown shaped like a pastry... It seems like I was uninvited by your lovely bride-to-be."

This song is allegedly written for Taylor's friend, who found herself in the position of having to watch the man she loved marry another woman. Taylor suggested to her friend that they crash the wedding and speak against it. While the women didn't go through with the stunt, Taylor thought about what she would do in such a situation. She sketched out her game plan in a song.

Taylor put herself in her friend's shoes when she wrote this. Taylor watches the 'bride' walking down the aisle. When she looks at the groom, she can tell that he wishes that she - Taylor - was the one in white, walking to him. Through her eyes, she pleads with him to run away with her. Finally, when the preacher asks if there are any objections, she gathers her courage, stands up, and looks at the groom. She disregards all the staring eyes, but she keeps her eyes on him. She pleads for him to come with her.

She ends the song talking about how the groom was glad she was around when he had to say his vows. He's thankful to her for saving her.

CHAPTER SIXTEEN

LOVE STORY AND SHAKESPEARE

The meaning of Taylor Swift's 'Love Story' is pretty straightforward, but I couldn't help analyzing it. It is one of my favourite songs and it is the one that made me fall in love with Taylor's music.

This song talks about a modern-day Romeo and Juliet, two forbidden lovers, meeting in secret. The song starts with Taylor, adopting Juliet's character, reminiscing about the first time she saw her 'Romeo.' She tells us that they were young when they both met, just like in Shakespeare's Romeo and Juliet, who were 16 and 13 when they met. She recalls that they met in the summer when she was leaning over the balcony.

She then refers to the Capulet's masked ball. She says she remembers the party where they met. She remembers the lights and the ball gowns. She says that 'Romeo' came up to her. She however didn't know that this boy would become her true love. She tells us that her father wanted them to stay away from each other.

She begs her 'Romeo' to take her away. She says that she will be waiting for him and they can run away together. She says that she would be his princess and he would be her prince. Here, Taylor deviates from Shakepeare's work. In his work, Romeo and Juliet weren't descended from royal blood.

In the bridge of the song, Taylor sings about how she got tired of waiting. She almost lost faith in her Romeo. She is unsure of where their relationship stands until 'Romeo' gets down on his knee and proposes to her. He tells Juliet that he smoothed things over with her father and he asks her to marry him.

The main difference between Taylor's Love Story and Shakespeare's Romeo and Juliet is the ending. Shakespeare ends his story in a tragedy, where both Romeo and Juliet die. Taylor however ends her story with the couple uniting against all odds.

CHAPTER SEVENTEEN

THIS IS ME TRYING

'This Is Me Trying' is - in my opinion - one of the most relatable songs in the Folklore album. I really relate to what she is trying to tell her fans. It's a song about vulnerability and insecurity. I feel like she wants everyone to know that everyone – including a famous singer like her – has insecurities. She wants us to acknowledge them.

"I've been having a hard time adjusting
I had the shiniest wheels, now they're rusting"

These show that people need time to adjust to a new situation or adjust to changes in life. I think the imagery with the wheels shows that even though a person was once at the top of their game, they can take some time to recover – without this being viewed as a fall from grace.

Pulled the car off the road to the lookout

"Could've followed my fears all the way down"

These lines tell us that it's easy to give up. We all would have faced a time when we knew it would all be so much easier if we just gave up. But, it's worth it to keep trying.

> *"They told me all of my cages were mental*
> *So I got wasted like all my potential"*

These mental cages refer to psychological problems. The wasted potential tells us that if we weren't affected psychologically, we would have been able to achieve so much more.

The chorus is very important here. When Taylor keeps telling us that she is still trying, she wants us to try as well. She doesn't want any of us to give up. (Believe it or not, Taylor does really care about her fans.)

Everyone, listen to Taylor, please. Do not give up! No matter how hard it seems, it will get better.

CHAPTER EIGHTEEN

I Can Do It With A Broken Heart

The day I wrote this was the day that Taylor's 11th album dropped. I was listening to the song 'I can do it with a broken heart' which inspired me to write this. This is about what I was feeling when I heard the song.

When I heard the first paragraph, I visualized a woman. She was a stereotypical blonde girl. Someone who was prom queen. Someone who was really popular and probably had everything she wanted. I pictured her as someone who took the love of my life away from me.

The chorus talks about a girl who can do it all. A girl who deals with a lot of problems but has to deal with them all on her own. She doesn't have anyone to turn to when she needs help. Someone tells the girl "You gotta fake it till you make it." I felt like that was a lesson to the girl, telling her not to share her sorrows with the world. Someone was telling her to let her successes speak for her and that she didn't have to answer to criticism. She had to smile in public even when she was really down and depressed.

Then, she remembers how her love left her. She remembers the promise he made her, that this love would last forever. Then, she realizes that he lied. I felt like the man left the girl for another girl. The girl was devastated by this and literally felt her heart crumble and shatter. However, she persists and meets people's expectations of her. She doesn't let this guy destroy all that she has worked for. She claims that she can do it all with a broken heart.

In the post-chorus, she says that she was very depressed but she acted happy. She put up an act that everyone believed. She admits to stalking her ex. (I mean, we all would, wouldn't we?) Her ex wants nothing to do with her. (Which is bound to hurt.) She says that she is productive, throughout her depression. Then she repeats that she can do it with a broken heart.

I feel like I really resonate with this girl. If she can do it, why can't I? This song both motivated me and broke my heart. It reminded me of things that I'd really like to forget. But, I'm determined not to let things get me down. I want my successes to speak for me, rather than be judged by my past.

CHAPTER NINETEEN

How Much Sad Did You Think I Had?

This is a lyric from 'So Long, London' from The Tortured Poets Department. To me, this line just confirms my claims that no one can know the amount of sadness that a person has in them.

> *"Thinking how much sad did you think I had*
> *Did you think I had in me?"*

I feel like this shows us that people can project one emotion outwardly and that people usually have no idea what is going on in the person's mind. This is something that people do a lot these days. People are afraid of showing others their emotions. They are worried that they are going to be judged. As I have mentioned in a lot of my previous posts, this is something that has to change.

These lines also show us that even pop stars like Taylor herself aren't always happy. They also put on a show. This song is allegedly about her break-up with Joe Alwyn. When this happened, she was on her legendary Eras Tour. She was facing a break-up after more than 5 years. She could have taken some time for herself, but she didn't. She just went on like nothing happened. This was a reality check for me.

I'm sure no one would have known what was going on in her head when she was performing. That's when these lines hit hard. I feel like no one really knows what you are going through but yourself. Until you let them in, I felt like this was a sign to let people know when I need help.

What I'm trying to say here is that you can't expect people to know what you're going through until you tell them what's wrong. I'm sure there are so many people out there who have your back. You probably have a lot of people who genuinely care for you and will want to help you. You just have to take a leap and trust them. Believe that they will be there for you and they will prove that they are. If they don't, that's your sign that they never really loved you.

CHAPTER TWENTY

JUST SAY "I LOVED YOU THE WAY THAT YOU WERE"

This is another lyric from The Tortured Poet's Department The Anthology. It's from the song 'Chloe or Sam or Sophia or Marcus.' The lyrics that I want to talk about read "If you wanna break my cold, cold heart just say, 'I loved you the way that you were.'"

These lines touched me. I feel like Taylor is telling us that her lover didn't like the way that she changed. She says that telling her that he loved the way that she was in the past is basically telling her that he doesn't love how she is now. I mean, she could have had her reasons for changing. She has the eyes of the world on her and wouldn't do things without thinking things through.

Yes. People change. If someone can't stick around to learn why, did they even love you to begin with? (I'm not commenting on Taylor's relationships here. I'm speaking in general.) I think that people have to be given the benefit of the doubt here. If some part of their character has changed

- something that has been constant for a long time - I believe that they must have undergone some life-altering experience. I don't think anyone has the right to judge you without knowing the whole story.

I'm very opinionated about this topic because I wasn't given the chance to explain myself when something similar happened to me. Or rather, I could say that people only wanted to see the old me. They would have done anything to see that side of me again. They didn't understand why I changed the way that I did. They were very quick to judge and hate.

When someone says that they loved the way that you were, it shows that they don't support your personal development. They don't understand that you very desperately need this change.

Wow! Taylor is making a philosopher out of me.

CHAPTER TWENTY-ONE

I Love You, It's Ruining My Life

Love is supposed to be legendary and epic. It should consume you and should give you what you want. That's what people believe at least. This is the most heartbreaking lyric from 'Fortnight.' It tells me that people have a lot of trouble noticing red flags in people. All they can see is the good. While that is good in some cases, a person should know what's wrong with their partner. They should be able to see that some things aren't right.

Let's look at the title of the song... Fortnight... which means 2 weeks. I feel like this song is talking about the damage that can be done in 2 weeks. Some things can't be taken back. Some relationships can't be fixed. I feel like the line I'm talking about (I love you, it's ruining my life) means that something horrible happened in just 2 weeks. The singer feels like she can't go back to the relationship. She feels like the love she has is ruining her.

This song talks about the effects of short-lived love. It proves that love is very strong, no matter how long it lasts or how toxic it is.

I think that people need to work on noticing red flags. This line sounds very fatalistic. It portrays love as deadly. Love isn't supposed to be that dangerous. True love should be effortless and easy. It shouldn't feel like it's killing you.

This line broke my heart and eventually drove me to tears. I felt like I had a love (not romantic. Remember, love can also be between friends) that ruined me similarly. This whole album is filled with very emotional and heartbreaking lyrics.

I really appreciate Taylor for writing these and helping me put my feelings into words.

CHAPTER TWENTY-TWO

ESCAPE IN ESCAPING

The title of this blog comes from the song 'The Bolter.' (Yes, by Taylor Swift.) Look at the lyric again. Like really look at it and feel it. Try to understand what it means. "There's escape in escaping."

Usually, escape is seen as cowardly. People who try to escape from situations are looked upon as weak. The society thinks that they can't handle themselves. They have gotten themselves into things that are too big for them. People should stop to look at the situation. Right?

Sometimes, the situation might have been toxic. This song talks about a relationship that has soured. In that case, a person has to get out of the relationship, i.e., escape. Here, escape is used as a noun first. It's used to represent a safe space. A place away from all the drama. A place where a person can be free from the problems that were in the relationship.

The word escaping is used as a verb as well. The most important thing is that it doesn't symbolize cowardice. It symbolizes self-preservation. The person is smart enough to get out of a toxic space. They can do what's best for them, without worrying about anyone else.

The reason that this line stood out to me is because these lines could be easily misinterpreted. It all depends on the perspective you are looking at it from. This is true for many situations. Perspective is really important.

CHAPTER TWENTY-THREE

LOSS OF MY LIFE

When you see the acronym 'loml', what would you think it means? Most people would quickly assume that it means 'love of my life.' When Taylor released the titles of her tracks, I knew loml wouldn't mean 'love of my life'. I thought it would mean 'lie of my life.' I didn't expect it to be 'loss of my life.'

I was mind-blown when I heard this lyric. Taylor says that losing this person was the greatest loss of her life. Throughout the album, she understands that it was for the best that the relationship ended. She might not be okay with it but she knows that she couldn't have gone on there.

A message that I take away from these lyrics is that you have to get out of a toxic situation. It will hurt you very much and might be the worst kind of heartbreak that you will ever face. As Taylor said, it will be the loss of your life. It will always be the biggest 'what if' that you will have.

There was another theory that suggested that loml might stand for 'lie of my life.' This was equally heartbreaking to think about. Imagine there is someone who promised you everything. They said that they would be with you forever. They said that you deserved the world and they assured that they would give it to you. Now, imagine that that person disappears from your life. They are gone. Poof. That would make everything that they promised you a lie. It's probably the best lie because you invested so much into it.

These are some of my interpretations of 'loml.' I'd like to make it known that these aren't proven facts. They are just things I felt when I was listening to the song.

CHAPTER TWENTY-FOUR

TOLERATE IT

"I made you my temple, my mural, my sky
Now I'm begging for footnotes in the story of your
life
Drawin' hearts in the byline
Always takin' up too much space or time"

These lyrics show us how much the speaker loved someone, but in the end, it wasn't enough. This is the story that I think these lyrics tell us.

She built her entire world around this guy. Hypothetically speaking, she cut off all her other contacts for him. She isolated herself just so she could spend enough time with him. She thought he deserved everything she had. Every cell in her body told her that he was the one. She made him her world.

In the end, she found out that he didn't love her as much. She was abandoned by him. He accused her of taking up too much of his time. This is really ironic, seeing as how she gave up her other friends for him. He should have been thankful for it, but instead, all he could see were her imperfections. She held these against her.

She now had to beg him for attention. Since she built her world around him, she had nowhere else to go. When he left her, her entire world fell into chaos.

CHAPTER TWENTY-FIVE

It's Mine Alone To Disgrace

The whole lyric reads 'I'll tell you something about my good name, it's mine alone to disgrace.' This tells us that no one can really talk behind your back or disgrace you without your permission.

What I would like to take away from this is pretty similar. No one can make you feel inferior without your permission. I mean think about it. Would you let someone disgrace you? Especially if you were sure that they were wrong. Obviously, you would stick up for yourself.

It's the same with feeling inferior. It's all in your own head. If you let other people make you feel that way, it means that there's a part of you that feels that way about yourself. You have to feel better about yourself and about your abilities. It helps to surround yourself with people who help you up instead of pushing you down. Don't give anyone the right or ability to hurt you. Remember that you are just as good as anyone else. Remind yourself that you deserve everything that you want.

Coming back to the original lyric now, no one can disgrace you, until you do something wrong. If you didn't do anything, you have nothing to fear. The opinion that people have about you depends on the way you carry yourself and handle situations. You don't need to answer to anyone.

CHAPTER TWENTY-SIX

I'm Damned If I Do Give A Damn What People Say

Yesss! You can't let anyone control you. No matter how many times I say this, it is never enough

The most important thing is that you know what you are doing. You don't have to explain everything to the whole world. The people who really matter in your life won't question you if you are firm in your resolve. Here, when I say question, I don't mean that they won't check up on you and make sure that you are alright. I mean that they won't judge you for making your own decisions. The relationships that you make are yours. The world might look at them differently. They might be wrong. You can't sit around correcting everyone. If you do, you won't realize that the time you have to actually be in the relationship that you are fighting for is gone.

It's your life guys. You have to live it how you want to. If you keep waiting for someone's approval, you are never going to get anything done. If you are clear about what you want, that should be enough. The thing is, someone is always going to have something to say. Someone is always going to try to put you down. If you keep listening to everything, you aren't going to get anywhere.

The title of this entry is actually a song lyric, from Lavender Haze. It's basically telling people not to worry too much about what other people have to say. It's telling us to live our lives the way we want to.

CHAPTER TWENTY-SEVEN

SPARKS FLY - THE STORY

Every time I hear the song Sparks Fly, a picture paints itself in my mind. I can visualize the things that are happening to the girl in the song. Through this post, I'm going to try to show you that same picture. Try to put yourself in the scene as you read.

You are a girl in New York. It's nighttime and the street is pretty much deserted. You see him approaching you. He is dressed in black from head to toe. His walk is masculine and lithe. He looks like a lion, stalking his prey. There's no way you can escape him. You have been ensnared in his gaze. Your inner conscience tells you he's probably bad news, but you know you are too far gone. You couldn't escape even if you wanted to. But, do you want to?

You blink once and as you open your eyes, he's standing right in front of you. There is a loud thunderclap. You want to glance up to see if it's about to rain, but you can't take your eyes off him. He's close enough to touch. You want to lean over and touch him, to make sure he's a real man and not a figment of your imagination. But, could your imagination really create something so perfect? The way he looks into your eyes makes you feel like he can read your mind. He's looking right into your soul curiously.

The rain starts drizzling and you both look at the sky. The rain gets heavier as your eyes meet again and he grabs your waist. He pulls you close and you can smell the perfume he's wearing. He dips you and kisses you as the rain pours all around. You can't feel anything except his lips against yours. As he lets you go, he smiles at you. When the smile meets his eyes, you feel butterflies in your stomach and his smile is as bright as fireworks in the night sky. You can't help but smile back at him.

His bright green eyes search yours for any hesitation. He finds none. There's still a part of you that's sane. It's telling you not to let yourself get sucked into this man's trap. He touches you gently and you feel your hair rise up. You have goosebumps all over your body. He traces his fingers languidly up and down your arm. You usually have a good sense of right and wrong. But, when it comes to him, there's no use keeping your guard up. You relish his touch, waiting, all the while, for him to kiss you again.

You run your fingers through his hair and it is softer than you ever imagined. He doesn't take his eyes off you. He takes your hand and leads you up a staircase. You find yourself going with him willingly. He leans over and whispers in your ear "I'm captivated by you, baby, like a fireworks show." You shiver with pleasure as he kisses you again. This time, fireworks go off in the background as he smiles. It's as if nature itself is a slave to his smile.

CHAPTER TWENTY-EIGHT

You Don't Get To Tell Me About Sad

This is another line from the Tortured Poet's Department. It's from the song 'Who's Afraid of Little Old Me' On the whole, this song tells us a story of a girl who wasn't really taken seriously. As the title of the song tells us, the world never thought that this girl could do anything. No one was afraid of her talents.

I feel like this line is telling us that everyone feels sorrow and grief in different ways. You can't make a person feel things in one particular way. Everyone has different ways of expressing emotions. It's telling us that no one can really tell you how to feel. Your emotions can't be controlled. You have the right to feel what you want, when and where you want to. No one can tell you not to do so.

Another lyric from the same song is 'You wouldn't last an hour in the asylum where they raised me.' This tells us that everyone's problems are their own. Everyone has their own past and skeletons in their closets. No one knows about what you have gone through, but you. And that's okay. You don't need to feel the need to make everyone understand what you have faced. (It's okay if you want to share it with a couple of people, but it doesn't need to public knowledge.)

So, since no one knows what's happening, they don't get to tell you how to feel. They can't tell you that you can't be upset. That's the main idea of this line. (In my opinion)

CHAPTER TWENTY-NINE

MEMORIES ARE VERSATILE

"And baby, I get mystified by how this city screams your name
And baby, I'm so terrified of if you ever walk away"

These lyrics are from 'Cornelia Street,' from the album,' Lover.'

Imagine you have an epic love. (When I say love, it doesn't have to be romantic. You can imagine a platonic love as well.) You have pretty much traveled all around the city with them. Everything around you is filled with memories that you guys share. You have been everywhere and done everything there is to do. You can't go anywhere without being reminded of them.

So, now what happens if that person leaves? Here, I don't necessarily mean a breakup or a fight. What if they move away? What would happen to you when you are left behind? First, let's imagine that you have parted on good terms. You promise each other to meet regularly. You tell yourself that you will be fine without them.

In reality, everything around you reminds you of them. You can't look at anything without memories flooding back. You miss them immensely. It's so hard to breathe. But, the good thing is that these memories are good. Once you get past the initial pain, you feel warm as you let the memories swarm your mind. Now, if you ended on bad terms, things would be different. The memories would never bring you comfort. The pain would never end. You wouldn't be able to function normally unless you leave. (Here, when I say leave, I mean move away.)

The lyric ends by saying 'I'd never walk Cornelia Street again.' The speaker says that if her love ever leaves, she will never be able to walk around the city (or street) again.

The point I'm trying to make here is that memories are versatile. You might have had a good time making them, but when you recall them, they could be good or bad. Good memories can also hurt. Bad memories can also offer you comfort sometimes. (You might feel relief that it's finally over.) It depends on how we remember moments.

CHAPTER THIRTY

LAST KISS

The bridge of this song is one of the most heartbreaking things that I have heard.

> "*So I'll watch your life in pictures like I used to watch you sleep*
> *And I feel you forget me like I used to feel you breathe*
> *And I'll keep up with our old friends just to ask them how you are*
> *I hope it's nice where you are*"

It tells us about the emotions that one feels after a break-up. Here, the speaker is obviously still in love with her ex-lover. But, unfortunately, she has to watch his life from a distance now. That breaks her heart. Another line in the song says 'I never thought we'd have a last kiss.' She truly believed that the relationship would last forever.

I'm sure this is something that everyone can relate to. How can you love someone without seeing a future with them? How can you let someone go without missing them to the point of insanity? Is it possible to skip the heartbreak and just go back to the way you used to be? I certainly don't think so.

I think that heartbreak is inevitable in any relationship. You can't get around the hurt that you feel. All you can do is console yourself with the thought that the person you love will have a better life without you. (Even if you still believe that you are perfect for them.)

I think you should simply cherish the relationship while it lasts. Once it's over, give yourself time to heal. Yes, it will be hard. But, you need to take time for yourself. Don't keep checking on the other person. You can wish them the best, but watching them from a distance will hurt. Seeing them with someone else will hurt. Don't let them hurt you.

CHAPTER THIRTY-ONE

KILL THE ONE YOU LOVE

"You know there's many different ways that you can kill the one you love
The slowest way is never loving them enough"

These lines are really very true. There are many ways that you can kill the one you love - or rather kill love itself. You can make someone lose all belief in love. You can make them lose all hope for their future. You can break their heart. You can send them into depression. You can hamper their relationships in the future. You can make them doubt themselves. You can make them feel like everything is their fault.

'The slowest way is never loving them enough.' You don't give them the love that they deserve. You can make them feel inferior. You can even make them feel like they don't deserve your love. But, no one has the right to make another person feel like they don't deserve love. Everyone deserves love. If you can't give them that - for whatever reason - that's on you. You shouldn't make them feel like they are unworthy. That can really hamper things that they aspire to do. Not just relationships, but their dreams as well. They might feel like they are incapable of doing anything.

If you can't love the other person, you should have the courage to tell them. Instead, if you're just leading them on, it will hurt more when the inevitable happens. No one deserves to be led on - no matter what reasons you tell yourself to justify your actions. If you are determined to kill the one you love, at least be kind in the way you do it. Don't be sadistic with them. They deserve better.

CHAPTER THIRTY-TWO

FIFTEEN

The song 'Fifteen' is a beautiful portrayal of a typical high school experience. It starts on the first day of high school, walking through the doors. The narrator is obviously very nervous and she is trying to stay out of everyone's way. She has loads of dreams. She has a lot that she wants to do. Being a typical teenager, she believes that she has everything figured out.

One of her little dreams was hoping to catch the eye of a senior boy. She wanted to be seen. (This is something that every teenage girl wants. Everyone wants to be seen and known.) The speaker tells us that when you're fifteen, you really believe in love. If someone tells you that they love you, you believe them without a doubt. She believes that she knows what she's doing.

The speaker talks about meeting her best friend by chance. All she did was sit next to this girl, and things just fell into place. Before she knew it, they were inseparable. Smash cut into her first date. Her mom was waiting to hear all about it. As any teenager would think, she thought that he was the one. She thought she was the one she would share her life with.

Up until now, the song is like a beautiful fairytale, where nothing could go wrong. Soon, she realized that there was more to life than dating a popular guy. She didn't know that when she was fifteen. All she wanted then was to be the object of someone's attraction and attention. She tells us that if she could go back in time, she would advise her younger self against this. She thought she would marry this guy someday, but she realized that she had bigger things to achieve.

The point of this song is to tell us that the things you experience during your teenage years aren't things that will last all throughout your life. However, we can see that the friendships you form are very important. Here, the speaker and her friend both cry together. This is a metaphor for facing problems together. Romantic relationships that you have during high school won't last. However, they will teach you things. Friendships on the other hand are very strong. This song is telling us to look for our dreams and to make sure that nothing gets in our way. This is what I think the song is trying to tell us.

CHAPTER THIRTY-THREE

'Cause He Really Knows Me

"*I want to wear his initial on a chain round my neck, chain round my neck*
Not because he owns me, but 'cause he really knows me."

This is a lyric that I can really understand. When you wear someone's initials, it doesn't mean that they own you. It doesn't mean you are theirs. It's not a symbol of ownership. It's a symbol that the initial you are wearing means something to you. It can be that of your best friend, your parents, your partner, or your own as well.

I think it's a big honour if someone wears your initials. It means that you have made a great impact on their lives. If they are wearing it, it obviously means that it's a positive impact that you made on them. It might not seem like much to you, but you probably did something that they really needed. You might have made them believe in themselves again. You might have boosted their confidence. You might have been their biggest supporter. You might have been the reason they succeeded in their endeavours. You might have listened to them when they needed someone to talk to. You might have been just the person they were waiting for.

Whatever you did, they are probably really thankful to you for what you did. They respect you immensely and that's something that doesn't go away easily.

You should really be honoured if someone chooses to wear your initials.

CHAPTER THIRTY-FOUR

THAT LINE

I was watching the All Too Well short film, directed by Taylor Swift when this thought struck me. Sometimes, there is a line that shouldn't be crossed. It might seem small to you, but once it's crossed, there's no going back from it.

There was this scene where the couple on screen were fighting. The guy asked her for her forgiveness and she accepted. But, look at the lyric that followed that scene. 'And I know it's long gone and there's nothing else I could do. I forget about you long enough to forget why I needed to.' Take a moment for the lyrics to sink in.

It doesn't matter that there was an apology or reconciliation. There's no way that they are going to look at each other the same way. They might share intimate moments again. But, it doesn't really matter. There's a break in their relationship. Things aren't going to be that easy again. The level of trust they place in each other won't be the same as before. There's always the possibility of hurt. There's the possibility of something similar happening again.

I believe that this is true in all relationships. Misunderstandings happen. It is possible to come back from them. You can be what you once were. But, there is a line that shouldn't be crossed. You can't come back from that. You will never trust the other person the way you did. There's no way to remedy this. No amount of apologies will fix it. You will close yourself off from the other person. No matter how much they try to fix things, it's just a waste of their energy and time. Everything they do will just remind you of that one incident.

Trust - or any relationship - is like a glass. Once it's been broken, it can't be fixed again. No matter what anyone tries.

CHAPTER THIRTY-FIVE

LET IT ONCE BE ME

> *"Please,*
> *I've been on my knees*
> *Change the prophecy*
> *Don't want money*
> *Just someone who wants my company*
> *Let it once be me*
> *Who do I have to speak to*
> *About if they can redo*
> *The prophecy"*

This particular line in the song 'The Prophecy' sang out to me. What I see here is a girl who was always second best. She was someone who put everyone else's needs before her own. She would do anything for someone she loved. She would sacrifice herself for someone she loves.

Yet, nothing she does is ever enough. Even though she prioritizes important people in her life, no one does the same for her. She is never anyone's first choice. She doesn't know what it's like to be prioritized. She doesn't know how to let anyone take care of her. However, she wants to know what that feels like.

Yes, she is a high maintenance. Yes, she does have some expectations. But, that doesn't mean that she doesn't need someone to be there for her. It doesn't mean that she doesn't secretly crave a bit of pampering from time to time. She is self-sufficient, but she needs some time to be small.

This girl wants to be chosen by someone. She wants to be prioritized. She craves someone who knows her inside out and loves her despite all her flaws. She wants someone to look past them and see her for who she truly is. She wants to be someone's first priority.

If you see a girl like this... someone craving this... someone who puts everyone before herself... prioritize her once in a while. She will thank you very much.

CHAPTER THIRTY-SIX

THAT'S THE WAY I LOVED YOU

Everyone has different ways of showing their love. That's why we have the whole idea of love languages. This song talks about a beautiful relationship.

The narrator is telling us about the various reasons she loved her guy. She tells us about all the reasons he was a gentleman. She says that she couldn't ask for anyone better. I'm sure a lot of us can relate to this. We feel like the person we are in a relationship with is the best person ever and that we could never have anything better than that person.

Then she reminisces about their relationship before they were together. (This is what I think is happening. I can't say this is what the song actually means.) She tells us that their relationship wasn't always as smooth as it is now. She tells us that there were ups and downs. She tells us that they had plenty of arguments. But, she tells us that the relationship was like a rollercoaster. It was scary and unexpected, but it was still magical and exciting. Again, I'm sure we can all relate to that. Relationships are hard until you settle into them. The important thing is that you get past the fear and realize that the relationship is worth the hardships and struggles that come with it.

Then, the narrator tells us how the guy fits into her family. Then, the song takes a dark turn. She tells us how the guy doesn't notice that she is hurting inside.

I, however, don't want to get into the dark side. I love this song and I don't want to think about the sombre ending.

ALL TOO WELL

There are a few lyrics in the song 'All Too Well Ten Minute Version' that stood out to me. The first one was 'And you call me up again just to break me like a promise, so casually cruel in the name of being honest.'

The second one is 'You kept me like a secret, but I kept you like an oath.'

These are lyrics that touch my heart in one way or another every time I listen to them. The second one especially. It talks about the difference in the level of commitment that two people have to each other. To one person, it's not very serious. To the second person - the narrator of the song - the amount of commitment that she shows towards her partner and their relationship is magnanimous.

Going back to the first lyric now, one aspect of the lyric is that honesty - or the truth - does hurt sometimes. Her partner - or rather her ex - says some things to her that are really cruel. But, in the end, he was being honest with her. Yes, you should be honest, but can't you make an effort to be kind - or even decent towards the other person? The other aspect is about just how much you can break a person - or how many times you can do so. One simple phone call had the power to break the narrator. That shows how much she has been broken in the past.

As I have said many times before... heartbreak is inevitable. Relationships do fall apart. But that doesn't give us the right to break another person. Every human being deserves basic respect and some amount of humane kindness.

CHAPTER THIRTY-EIGHT

THE VERY FIRST NIGHT

In my opinion, this song is pretty much a tribute to someone who the narrator misses more than anything. 'The Very First Night' refers to the first night that the pair spent apart. I think it's the night after they fell in love. They couldn't stay together. That was the moment that she knew how much she really loved the other person. It's obvious that you can't miss someone you don't love. To miss someone after knowing them for a short period of time is a sign of how deep the love is.

Over the course of the song, the narrator says that she doesn't let her friends know that she's brokenhearted after the relationship ended. She keeps it all to herself. She lets them believe that she is happy and content with her life when in reality, she's pretty heartbroken and lonely. The love she shared with this person was surprising. They fell in love unexpectedly. No one expected them to fall in love. In my opinion, that's true in every relationship. Relationships are usually found where you least expect them to be. You might not want to feel what you feel, but it's inevitable.

The narrator goes on to reminisce on old memories. She keeps wishing she could go back in time when things were better. She wants the other person to know how much he meant to her. She wants him to know how much she misses him.

Since the narrator is trying to hide her feelings, her friends don't know how much she misses him. I can empathize with that. No one can really understand just how much you miss another person. This is because no one but you knows the extent of your relationship with one another. No one knows exactly how much they mean to you. No one knows exactly what you have shared with each other. And that's okay. Not everything is meant to be shared.

The downside is that no one knows what losing them does to you (which makes them believe you are creating a lot of drama over something trival).

CHAPTER THIRTY-NINE

FEARLESS

There's a picture that the chorus of this song paints in my head. The chorus goes 'Cause I don't know how it gets better than this. You take my hand and drive me head first. Fearless. And I don't know why but with you I'd dance in a storm in my best dress. Fearless.'

So here it goes. There's a girl who's usually very prim and proper. She prefers to stay indoors. She sticks to things she is familiar with and she doesn't regret it. She is the last person you would expect to be outdoors. But, for this one guy, she would set aside her morals. She would do anything for him.

This reminds me a bit of an argument between Damon and Elena from The Vampire Diaries. Elena says that she sets aside her morals and everything that she believes in for Damon. Now, this might seem toxic, but in the song, this just shows how pure the love between the two people is.

This perfect girl is willing to dance in a storm in her best dress. It shows that she cares for the guy more than she cares for the dress. Now I don't think the dress literally means a dress. I think it's a metaphor. The girl is telling us how she would put the guy first and how she would prioritize him over other things that she likes - here, the dress. She tells us that she would sacrifice 'the dress' for the boy.

It shows how much she loves him. It shows that she is willing to change herself because she thinks that he is worth it. Now, some change in a new relationship is perfectly fine. The thing to remember is to make sure not to lose your own individuality. You can sacrifice certain things for your partner but you have to remember that you are still your own person. You can't give up everything you love for them. There has to be a middle ground.

CHAPTER FORTY

CHAMPAGNE PROBLEMS

I admit, I'm not an Evermore fan. But, there were a few lines from this song that stood out and demanded my attention.

"I was never ready, so I watch you go."

This lyric shows us that we can't keep waiting for the opportune moment. We have to take things by storm. If we keep waiting, we might lose something that we love. We might never be ready for what could happen. But, we can't let that stop us from trying. You'll never know what could happen if you never try. Here, the lyric refers to a relationship. The narrator wasn't ready to confess her feelings for the other person, so she ended up losing him.

The beginning of the song talks about how the narrator broke someone's heart. She tells us how he left him stranded, and how she let go of him while dancing. She says...

"Your heart was glass, I dropped it."

This line reminds me of something someone used to tell me. "Trust is like a broken glass. Once it's broken it can't be fixed again," he said. Hearts are similar. After a heartbreak, it's really hard to find your normal again. It's hard to find your sense of equilibrium. The person who broke your heart might still be your soft spot. You might find yourself making excuses for them. But, your heart is still broken. You won't be able to trust them the way you did before.

This song is a story about the repercussions that a failed relationship has - not only on the two people involved but on their families as well. It talks about heartbreak and rejection. It initially doesn't look like a song that has a lot of depth, but when you really look into it, you can see the hurt that the writer is trying to convey.

CHAPTER FORTY-ONE

TEENAGE LOVE TAUGHT YOU THERE'S GOOD IN GOODBYE

Ohh yes. I'm sure we all have had our fair share of teenage love. I'm sure we believed that it would last forever.

Look back and remember the endless drama that followed. Teenagers don't really know what love is. They just love the idea of love. It's nothing more than infatuation. Yet, when one experiences it, it seems like it would last forever. There was probably a lot of sneaking around. You thought that it was the joy of the first love.

I'm sure there were some good parts. You probably learned what to expect in the future. You learned what you needed. You learned what to avoid. You learned about your boundaries. You discovered new sides of yourself. You figured out what you would and wouldn't do for another person. It set you on a path of self-discovery. There was also an inevitable heartbreak when you swore off dating.

You thought your life would never be the same again. You felt like you would never get over it. Spoiler alert... you did. And guess what? You became better than you ever were before.

Now, let's look at what the lyric is telling us... there's good in goodbye. Once you learn that you aren't good for each other, staying together is senseless. Teenage love is something that teaches you what life is like. It shows you that not all that glitters is gold. There is something good that comes out of saying goodbye to someone. You get to rediscover yourself. Isn't that just amazing?

CHAPTER FORTY-TWO

AM I ALLOWED TO CRY?

Why do you need to ask for permission to cry? To me, that shows the sorry state of today's world. In this world, people don't have the freedom to feel emotion - not only sadness. The world is so cruel these days.

Showing emotion is one of the most basic things. It's horrible that people can't show emotion without permission. I mean, why do you need to ask whether you are allowed to feel? It's not only sadness. If a person is happy in public (and showing it), people have to ask why. It's not just that they are curious, they are jealous. They are jealous that they aren't happy. Why can't someone just be genuinely happy for another person? The world is so competitive. No one really wishes the best for you.

The opposite thing happens when you are upset. People watching are really happy to see that you are upset. That's just plain evil. If someone is upset, one's instinct should be to ask what's wrong and to try to make them feel better.

There are only a few people in your life who will feel your emotions with you. By that, I mean only a few people will empathize with you. They will stay to watch your highs and lows. They won't leave when things get hard. They will have your back and they will celebrate with you when you succeed. Look for those people. Once you find them, don't lose them, They are the greatest treasure you will ever have.

CHAPTER FORTY-THREE

WHO'S AFRAID OF LITTLE OLD ME?

This is the title of a song from The Tortured Poets Department. To me, it feels like the singer is telling us that people have a habit of underestimating her.

I'm sure a lot of people feel like their abilities are often underestimated. People don't realize what you are capable of until you prove it. It's not enough to just say something. You have to show the world that you can do it. That's the only way you will earn their respect.

Here, the narrator is a monster or witch descending on a town who has shamed her. This town doesn't fear or respect her. She is trying to change that. She wants to show them just what she is capable of and terrorizes the town.

"So I leap from the gallows and I levitate down your street. Crash the party like a record scratch as I scream..."

The picture this creates in my mind is one of a devilish figure. She is all ready to be executed when she breaks her bonds and jumps onto the street. There's a party, where people are celebrating her capture. She breaks through the door and enters the room, cocks her head, and grins at the crowd, evil shining in her eyes. She is determined to wreak havoc upon those who wronged her.

The message that the song is giving us is that everyone is powerful and dangerous in their own way. We shouldn't think otherwise, it might have disastrous consequences.

CHAPTER FORTY-FOUR

Why Is Reading So Important?

I'm not going to say something philosophical like "Today's readers are tomorrow's leaders." Instead, I'm going to talk about why I love reading and why I think it's important.

I started reading at a very young age and have always felt like books were my constant companion. They were my ticket to escape reality. I strongly believe that reading allows you to enter a world that you could never imagine existed. They make you forget everything else and let you lose yourself in the story. My favourite type of book is one written from the first-person perspective.

Here, you become the character. You become the protagonist. The whole world revolves around YOU! You get to live the story, an epic adventure or intimate romance. Reading also helps improve your vocabulary and your general knowledge. I mean, I wouldn't have known half the things I do if I didn't read.

Watching the mistakes that the characters in the story make helps make sure you don't make the same mistakes. You can learn from them and grow with them. When you identify with the characters, you learn more about yourself.

Reading can help you identify your flaws and strengths. But, beware, they can make you fall for morally grey men. Reading also enhances your creative ability. It's always been my dream to publish a book and to see my name on the cover of a book. I realize that the only way I can achieve that is if I have a high creative thinking capacity, which reading helps me gain.

Reading has played a vital role in my life and I would really encourage everyone to read more. It can truly add something to your life that you never realized you were lacking.

CHAPTER FORTY-FIVE

How To Start Writing?

As an upcoming writer, I remember how hard it was to start writing. There is the constant fear of worrying that people won't like your writing. It's easy to think of a single scene but hard to draft a whole story. Here's what I did.

The first thing I did was decide on my theme and genre. I was very clear that I wanted to write fiction – since I was an avid fiction reader. The most important part about a theme is making sure you do your research. You have to know enough about your theme that you can build an entire book. For example, if you want to write about Greek Mythology, you have to know all about the gods and the Greek story of creation. You can't make silly mistakes with the basic facts.

The next step is deciding who your main character will be. If you are a female writer and your main character is a boy, you have to know how a boy thinks and acts and vice versa. You also have to name your character. Bonus points if your name is related to your theme.

Next, you have to figure out the storyline. You have to decide on the conflict and think about how the character gets from the beginning to the conflict to the end. You also have to have a clear distinction between the protagonist and antagonist.

Then, you need to decide on the perspective that you want to tell the story from. My favourite perspective is the first-person singular. I feel like it makes the reader feel more involved in the story.

Then, you need to decide how to start your story. In my opinion, the beginning of the story is the most important part. A reader decides if they want to keep reading or not.

These are my tips on how to start writing. Go for it! Get started!

CHAPTER FORTY-SIX

What Do Readers Expect In A Fiction Book?

The first thing that readers expect in a fiction book is something completely unexpected. That's right, people expect the unexpected. They are looking for surprises and twists. People want suspense. They want to be kept on the edge of their proverbial seats, wondering what's going to happen next.

Readers also want a character that they can connect with. The main character shouldn't be a perfect person. He or she has to have some kind of fatal flaw upon which the fate of the world rests. This raises the stakes and gets the reader more involved in the story.

Another significant expectation of readers is an escape. People read to escape their reality. A fiction or fantasy novel should be able to achieve that. A writer should be able to transport the reader to a new world where they can forget themselves and let themselves be immersed in the story.

Certain readers also want some intellectual challenges. This is also a way of escaping reality. They think that the problems or challenges in the story are easier to solve than those in real life.

One thing that I expect from a book is some kind of knowledge. When I read, I want to learn something new. Books are a great source of general knowledge. For example, when I'm reading Rick Riordan, I want to learn something new about mythology.

The first thing I look for before choosing a book is the genre. Writers have to be clear on their genre and theme. The first few sentences are what really attract the audience, like flies to honey.

These are just what I expect from a good fiction book (or my idea of a good fiction book). Different people expect different things.

CHAPTER FORTY-SEVEN

THE MEANS TO ATTAIN A HAPPY LIFE

The day I wrote this, the Head of my Department delivered an interesting lecture about 'The Means to Attain a Happy Life' by Henry Howard, the Earl of Surrey. She inspired me to write about my views of the poem and what I took from it.

Howard starts by claiming that a happy life is obtained when we obtain money without effort. I believe that some easy money is good in the beginning, to get a person on his or her feet, but later, it leads to laziness. A person needs something to occupy their time. If money is readily available, their mental and physical capabilities will decline.

He then speaks about suitable companionship. He claims that a friendship shouldn't have any conflicts and friends shouldn't hold grudges against each other. I believe that true friendship can not exist without some degree of conflict. In the end, what matters is that the two companions don't abandon each other and come back together once their conflict is resolved.

Howard then says a happy life is one without disease and a proper diet. He believes that health is important to lead a happy life, which I agree with. He also says that a good and faithful wife will lead to a man having a happy life.

My professor advised us girls to remain calm in the face of conflict. She told us that our words were very powerful and that we should be very careful with them. "Girls, be silent and patient. Correct them with love. Argumentative wives can be dangerous," she said. I remember scoffing at this statement. I think we are not obliged to remain calm all the time. The situation and problem at hand are important determining factors.

Howard concluded his poem by telling us not to wish for death nor to fear it. I agree with this completely. Death is indeed inevitable and will come for us all. However, we shouldn't covet it before our time. This was one of the few poems that I delved into and it was surely worth it. Howard's views were informative and his writing shows that he believed everything he said.

In the end, I believe that moderation is the key. Too much of a good thing is bad and on the other hand, we need some pleasure and happiness in life.

CHAPTER FORTY-EIGHT

POSSESSIVENESS, PROTECTIVENESS AND BEING TERRITORIAL

These are three words that are often used but the meaning behind them might not be clear. They are all interconnected though.

Being possessive - according to the dictionary - means that you always demand someone's total attention and love. Being protective means that you would do anything to keep someone safe. Being territorial means that you are protective over your relationship with someone.

One difference I notice between being possessive and being territorial is that one is usually territorial over something that one already has. On the other hand, possessiveness might be associated with something that one covets. More logically, being territorial can be related to space or material objects while being possessive can be related to a person.

Here's the thing... all these things can become toxic if they are allowed to go overboard. There is naturally going to be possessiveness in any relationship, but what matters is that there is also trust present. You have to know that there's no way that you can keep a person all to yourself. That's how you get around being extremely territorial.

Then there is protectiveness. Okay, let's face it. That is totally natural as well. Think about it. You are going to be protective over anyone you love. You wouldn't want anything to harm them. You would want to keep them safe. Sometimes, you might think that they are safest with you. That is when you may start feeling possessive. You might think that you are best for them. You might be, but that doesn't give you the right to keep them away from the world - or other people.

The important thing to remember is balance. If not, the consequences could be disastrous.

CHAPTER FORTY-NINE

HOW TO READ EFFECTIVELY

I am an avid reader, as I've mentioned before. I've noticed how a lot of people have trouble reading – even books mentioned in the syllabus. In my opinion, reading is not a passive activity and it requires energy and attention.

I think the reason that people aren't able to concentrate on reading is that they aren't interested. I believe that you can't read something that you don't like. The theme of the book is also important. Certain things appeal to certain people. For example, I can read anything with a supernatural theme.

The books in the syllabus however aren't really appealing to modern readers (in my opinion). You need a lot of persistence to sit through a book like Jane Eyre. (It's worth it, but the storyline is slow. Yeah, I know it's a classic.)

One of my tips for reading effectively is to start reading with a positive attitude. You have to believe that you will like the book before you even open it. You also have to be determined to finish reading it. Set a target for the number of pages that you want to finish in a day – make sure it is reasonable. Set aside some time every day to read.

As I mentioned earlier, reading isn't a passive activity. You have to be involved in the book. Put yourself in the shoes of the main character. Imagine that you are in the story and try to look for tools like foreshadowing. Try to predict what the characters are going to do next. Focus on the development the characters go through. Be sure to know the stakes the characters have in the plot and their relationships with each other.

Reading isn't hard, you just need the right frame of mind!

CHAPTER FIFTY

ANNA IS AN EMOTION

Brother is a word, but Anna is an emotion.

I agree with this very much. I have 3 older brothers, but I can't think of a time where they have actually been what a brother is supposed to be.

One really important thing to remember is that 'Anna' doesn't have to be someone with whom you share blood. It's someone you choose to respect and admire. It doesn't matter whether or not you call them 'Anna.' What matters is that you make sure that they know how much they mean to you. What matters is that know how much you respect and admire and look up to them.

Yes, you usually call a guy who's older than you this way. But think about it, auto Anna, tea-stall Anna, etc. They all have some sort of emotion attached to them. The auto driver Anna makes sure you reach your destination safely. "Take care and be safe," some of them say as they drop you off. The tea-stall Anna makes sure you have enough to eat. "Do you want anything else?" they ask. Obviously, you aren't going to divulge all your secrets to them, but when they ask you, you feel a small sense of belongingness. (I'm not saying the world doesn't have bad people. You do have to be careful.)

To me, the word Anna is associated with safety - emotional, physical, etc. (Which is why I don't call just anyone "Anna".) There are no strings attached and it's unconditional. There is blind trust and the belief that he won't abandon me. There's the faith that he has my back. Anna is someone I call out for when I'm in need, whether I'm happy or sad. I don't call many people that way. I don't trust many people with my emotions, but once I say the word "Anna," there's no going back.

Anna stands beyond the word brother, especially now that blood-related brothers don't care much. (I'm not trying to throw shade on anyone here). He is someone who makes you feel like you can do it. They are your biggest supporter and will celebrate your successes. He will try to ensure we don't make the same mistakes they did.

You can consider anyone your brother, but Anna is something different. Anyone can be your brother, but Anna reciprocates the love that you show and respects that bond.

Anna... Thank you for being my big brother. Thank you for choosing to do so. (I could keep going but I'm not going to.) Thank you to all the big brothers out there.

CHAPTER FIFTY-ONE

A Tribute To My Seniors

Before I start, I'd like to say that this is a very personal post, dedicated to a few very special individuals. Anderlin, Sharan, Shane, and Mugunthan. Technically they are my seniors, but they have become something more. These guys are the reason I made it through the year and have become irreplaceable brother figures to me. I may not call them 'Anna,' but the respect they earned from me is immeasurable.

I still remember the first time I saw them. I was at an ethnic walk practice session. It was only my second day there and I wasn't very confident yet. The four of them weren't around on the first day of practice. That's when they arrived. They appeared, walking in a straight line. They looked so majestic and powerful that they scared me. They came to stand in front of me and I remember chills running down my spine. None of them were laughing at the moment (you're not allowed to laugh or smile during an ethnic walk.) I was so intimidated by them. There aren't words to describe how I felt when I saw them showcasing their walks.

Once I got to know them, I found out how amazing they are. My initial fear vanished almost instantly. I realized that they might have looked scary once, but on the inside, they were marshmallow-soft. They each taught me a lot of valuable lessons. Over the year, I've spent a lot of time with them and they are undoubtedly the best part of my year. They made my year memorable and they each deserve to be celebrated with pride.

Mugunthan was always very jovial, no matter how much I teased him. He taught me to look at the bright side of things. He was the first one of them I talked to. He put me at ease with his causal smile.

Shane earned my respect instantly since he looked a lot like one of my cousin brothers. He was always really busy but was very patient and calm (as far as I know.) He commanded respect from everyone he spoke to. He looks like someone who is not really approachable but he is one of the best guys in his class. He soon became someone I idolized.

Sharan is someone whose love language is messing around with me. My favourite thing to do with him was to call him evil – which I do twice a day. However, he stood up for me when I needed it the most, which I will always be grateful for. He is constantly teasing me but it just improves my resilience. One of my favourite memories with him is riding a bike. He taught me how to be strong. His cool and laid-back nature is something I admire very much.

Saving the best for last, Anderlin. Words can't express the gratitude and affection I have for him. He was the one person who had my back all year. He became the brother that I always dreamt of having. He helped me settle into college. He built me back up piece by piece when I broke down. He is very patient and understanding. Never has he given me any reason to doubt him. He makes me feel safe in his presence. He taught me what blind trust felt like. He taught me about self-love and how important it was. He made me feel comfortable in my own skin. He is the person I look up to the most, and I always will.

The sight of them arriving at their farewell fete is something I can never erase from my mind. They appeared radiating power, just like the first time I saw them. I had déjà vu as I laid eyes on them. I was taken back to the beginning of the year. The only difference was that I wasn't afraid anymore. They took my breath away and brought tears to my eyes.

I can't end this tribute without mentioning another one of my idols, Harish. He was my mentor for the ethnic walk and is one of the most stylish guys I know. His patience and ability to teach is something I really admire and respect.

Thank you guys for making this year so special. I will never forget you all.

MNEMOSYNE 2024

Mnemosyne is my department's annual intercollegiate fest, for those of you who don't know. My journey started when I joined the volunteering committee and went on to volunteer to be a convenor. A while later, our ELF chairperson announced the list of convenors. I was disappointed to see that some other girls from my class were selected but I wasn't. I was disappointed because I had been putting a lot of effort into events throughout the year. I later found out that my best friend had already announced that he wanted me to volunteer for the event he was convening (spell bee). I forgot my disappointment and was overjoyed to work with him. I soon found out that the girl who was supposed to be the second convenor didn't want to do it. I was standing quietly next to some of my seniors as they were deciding who the other person should be. One of them looked at me and asked "Do you want to do it?" I nodded enthusiastically, hiding my joy.

My friend and I put a lot of effort into preparing for our event. We found out that there wasn't going to be a judge and that it was on us to handle things. The pressure was on!

The day of the event arrived and I felt unprepared. I was nervous and wasn't sure if I would be able to pull it off. My friend assured me that I could do it.

There were only a few participants on the first day of our event. I was thankful for that. It helped me get the hang of things and it showed me what to expect the next day. On the second day, there was a lot of confusion. My friend and I set up base at the registration desk, determined to take care of our event ourselves, not wanting to leave anything to the last minute. Even though there were people on the registration committee, we sat there to handle our event's registration. There was also a conflict with the timing and the venue of our event. We tried our best to remain calm throughout. We had double the participants the next day – not many though. We weren't able to execute the event as we had planned earlier but we made the best of what we had. My friend and I breathed a huge sigh of relief when the event ended. I collapsed and lay flat on the floor, laughing. I think the event was a success, irrespective of the number of participants and all the other conflicts we faced.

The experience taught me what happens behind the scenes of all the events I've attended throughout the year.

CHAPTER FIFTY-THREE

My Mountain

My favourite spot to hang out with my best friend is at the edge of a mountain in Tambaram. I don't want to mention the location to protect the serene beauty of the place. It's a 10-minute drive away from the MCC campus to the bottom of the mountain. It takes about 15 minutes to climb to the top. (Well, that depends on your stamina. It takes me around 15 minutes.) The climb is hard and can leave you breathless, but the experience you get at the top is unbelievable.

My friend and I believe that the climb is worth it. At the top, there is a temple, past which there is an outcropping of rocks. Luckily, there are some trees that provide shade and an occasional breeze up there.

The view is one of the best parts of it. You can see for miles from the vantage point. There are a lot of buildings and you can also see planes going in for a landing. There is also a water body there (we aren't sure which one it is yet.)

My favourite thing about this mountain is the peace being there gives us. We barely notice time passing up there. It's where we've had some of our most serious and open discussions. It's where I usually see my friend's true self. We are rarely disturbed up there and I feel like that gives us a chance to open up to each other. It offers us a place where we aren't afraid of judgment and can just be ourselves.

I'm really thankful I heard of this place and I'm thankful to it for everything it has given me.

CHAPTER FIFTY-FOUR

THE GUYS

Hanging out with 'the guys' is really amazing. Let me tell you about it.

For starters, they are not judgemental. You can tell them whatever you want to without having to worry about them looking at you differently. You don't have to worry that their perspective of you would change. Secondarily, you are very very safe with them. (I was hanging out with my brother and his friends. They pretty much adopted me.) This aspect is especially important if you are clumsy (like me). Third, they are really good listeners. Sometimes, girls are judgemental. They might pretend to care about you when you talk to them, but they might be glad that you are going through these problems.

(The next few things I want to mention might be trivial.)

Fourth, you don't have to worry about food getting wasted. If you get full, they'll finish your food for you. If you don't like what you ordered, the same principles apply. They also make sure that you eat. (Read: you will be force-fed if you haven't had a proper meal - their definition of proper is different from yours.) Fifth, you don't have to carry anything. They will carry your things - yes, your handbag as well if you ask nicely. Sixth, you can get all the pictures you want. (The guys I hang out with are pretty good at taking a whole bunch of good pictures of me.)

You can also learn a lot about life from them. The stories they tell you and the experiences that they share can show you that your problems are pretty minor. Their experiences teach you what to do and what not to do. The best part is that they aren't trying to preach to you.

These are just some of the many things that I noticed over the past 2 days. I'm sure there are a lot more things you can experience with the guys and there are many points that I forgot to mention.

CHAPTER FIFTY-FIVE

HE WHO MUST NOT BE NAMED

This post is meant for a person who toughened me up through my first year of college. (No it's not someone I mention often.)

This guy was there for me when I was at my lowest. I was sobbing my heart out one afternoon. All I did was call him and he rushed over. He sat by me, trying to make me smile, trying to distract me. When I started shivering, he pressed his leg against mine, trying to make it stop. (It didn't.) At the time, I couldn't think clearly enough to be thankful for him. Having him there made all the difference.

There was another time I needed him equally as much. It was a different situation and a bit more serious. Even though he didn't agree with me completely, he didn't sacrifice me. (By that I mean that he didn't change sides. He continued to stay by my side.)

He even let me play Barbie-doll with him. He sat still as I had the time of my life. (There was an event in college for which I helped him with some makeup.)

Throughout the year, one of his favourite things to do with me was to tease me. That was the way he greeted me.

Yes, at times it did provoke me. But, looking back on it, I just feel like he was doing his best to toughen me up. (It was his love language.)

Now that I don't see him often, I find myself longing for his playful teasing.

The point of this post isn't just to thank him, or to reminisce. It's to remind everyone that one person can make a huge effect on you. It's not just about who is always by your side (that doesn't mean you should forget those people.) It's about who showed up when you needed them the most and has continued to be someone you can rely on. You know that they will have your back and you can go to them without hesitation.

CHAPTER FIFTY-SIX

The Story Of How I Drove My Friend Home

Before that day, I'd only driven 2 bikes – yes, the ones with gears. The first time was in a secluded location, so I wasn't in danger of crashing into anything or falling. The second time was a Pulsar NS200, which I managed not to crash either. The second time didn't really count, my friend was the one doing the driving. I was sitting in front of him, pretending to hold on to the throttle (I think that's what it's called) like a little kid.

My best friend and I have had a running joke of me driving him home. I finally got to put my words into action. I persuaded my friend to pull over after we were off the main road. He obliged and let me get on in front of him. He reminded me of the controls – the clutch, gear shift, throttle, and the brakes.

"Remember to only use the back brake!" he instructed. That was a point of conflict for me. I remember reading Twilight, where Jake tells Bella that the back brake is dangerous and to only use the brake with her hand. He had previously explained the reason behind his words to me and I decided to trust him. I soon realized that using my leg to brake made me lose balance. "Just use your hand for now," he conceded grudgingly.

I managed not to crash or drop the bike. However, the bike did stop a couple of times. (I forgot to change the gear according to the speed.) I'm determined to learn how to do this flawlessly within the week.

Overall, I was really proud that I could actually drive my friend home. I'm also really thankful to him for trusting me enough to sit behind me. I'd also like to take a moment to let everyone know that he was a really patient teacher. He didn't lose his cool when the bike turned off or when I used the 'wrong' break.

PS – I apologize if any of the vocabulary I used above is wrong. I love bike rides and I want to learn how to properly drive one, but I'm not good with technical terms. *Contrite emoji*

CHAPTER FIFTY-SEVEN

SOMEONE TO TALK TO

Sometimes all you need is someone to talk to. You don't need to know them well. They don't need to be very familiar with you. That might make it easier for you. When you talk to someone you aren't close to, you feel like they won't judge you for not being yourself, because they don't know what your true self really looks like. You can just open yourself up to them.

When you start sharing your problems with someone, you feel like they are less daunting. You might not be looking for a solution to your problems. All you crave is someone who will take the time to listen to you. Unfortunately, that's hard to come by these days. People usually end up patronizing you. Finding someone who simply offers support is something that's really special and rare. After you talk to someone, you feel lighter. You feel like someone has heard your cries for help. Someone has heard what you have to say. You feel peace after being able to express yourself. For a little while, you forget about everything that has happened.

If you feel like you are drifting, look for someone you can talk to. Remember that you are never really alone. Help can be found in the most surprising places.

If you think someone needs help, go ask them. Don't hesitate. You never know the effect you might have on them. You might be just who they need.

CHAPTER FIFTY-EIGHT

MY INSPIRATION

Everyone has someone whom they idolize. To me, my inspiration is someone very close to me. Without them, I would never have been able to write all these blogs. No. It's not Taylor Swift. She might have given me content and material to write about, but there is someone else whom I idolize above all.

They don't realize that they are worth being idolized, no matter how many times I tell them. I say that they inspire me because they gave me the confidence to keep writing, no matter how many negative comments I received. They made sure I kept writing. Many of my posts are based on my experiences with them, things they told me, or things that I told them.

The best part about my source of inspiration is that they aren't a big famous celebrity. They are just another person who encourages me. If I had chosen a celebrity to idolize, they might have let me down someday. They might have changed their beliefs. I can trust that this won't happen with my inspiration. The best part is that they will continue to be a great source of inspiration for me through all my endeavors.

This person is someone who showed me who I want to be in a couple of years. They taught me how to handle situations. Their determination, resilience, versatility, kindness, and compassion (I could keep going on) are some things that I admire. They helped me through dark times as my guiding light and inspired me to help other people. They are more than just my source of inspiration. They are my safe space. They let me brainstorm with them and encouraged me to express myself. I repeat myself when I say that if it wasn't for them, I would not have been able to write these blogs.

Thank you... (you know who you are)

CHAPTER FIFTY-NINE

The Faces People Wear

Before I start, I'd like to let everyone know that I'm going to use gender-neutral pronouns in this post to protect the identity of the person I'm talking about. I've been observing a person closely for a while now and have noticed how they have different faces in front of different people.

For example, in front of me, they are one of the most sensitive and caring individuals I have met. They are open, kind, gentle, attentive and honest. They share things with me and are pleased to be in my company. When they are with their classmates, they usually come across as sullen and unresponsive. Around friends, they are a little less reserved but are still not the person I am familiar with. The way they relate to me in front of their friends is also different. I noticed how their entire personality changes depending on who they are with. The person I know isn't the same one other people see.

I took some time to ponder about why this could be and realized that I do the same thing too. One of my classmates told me that I'm childish and vulnerable around one person, but not in front of other people. I know that it's true and thought about why this happened.

I figured out that it depends on comfort and safety. Your inner child comes out around people you are comfortable with. Your inner child feels safe around them. It's the faith that you're not going to be judged for your actions that brings out who you actually are. In today's world, people are afraid to show their true colours, worried that they will be laughed at or judged.

It's our fault that we don't give people the space to be themselves. It's our fault that they have to hide who they are. We – on the whole – have to work on being more accepting.

CHAPTER SIXTY

EMBRACING YOURSELF

A problem that a lot of people have these days is embracing themselves. People are constantly seeking approval from others to make themselves feel good. This has to stop. People should stop looking to others to make themselves happy. Happiness should come from within.

There's always going to be someone who doesn't like you. If you keep listening to everyone, all you're going to end up doing is ruining your own peace of mind. No one is perfect. You just need to know and embrace your flaws and imperfections instead of denying them. Get to know yourself. Reflect on what makes you you. Make sure you understand what is important to you, and prioritize them. Remember to take care of yourself.

Surround yourself with positive people. Good company can make all the difference. Pick people who celebrate your unique qualities instead of those who critique and judge you at every turn. Remember that everyone is different. Don't compare yourself with others. Be kind to yourself and don't put too much pressure on your own mind.

Embracing yourself can also mean reducing your posts on social media. People can't help but say negative things to you, which will lead to you losing your peace. Keep your happiness to yourself and celebrate it with your loved ones. You don't need to show anyone that you are happy.

Remember that you are beautiful and amazing, no matter what anyone else says. Xoxo.

CHAPTER SIXTY-ONE

It's Okay To Be Vulnerable

Being vulnerable is often misunderstood as being weak. Vulnerability is a sign of feeling safe and secure. When we embrace vulnerability, other people see our true selves. Being yourself helps build better relationships.

People are scared to be vulnerable. They are worried that they will ridiculed or judged. Vulnerability is rare. People don't really show their true selves to others. People should know that it's okay to show they are vulnerable - after all, it is a sign of being human. Humans are supposed to have emotions and they are allowed to feel. Right?

The world is cruel. It misjudges vulnerability as a weakness. In my opinion, feeling secure enough to be vulnerable is actually a sign that you are emotionally and mentally strong. You don't have to be vulnerable in front of everyone, but at the same time, you can't keep all of your emotions to yourself. It's okay to be insecure sometimes. It's okay to be afraid of the scary possibilities of the future.

Something I always tell my best friend is that it's okay to let your emotions get out of hand sometimes. It's okay to let your emotions control you. It's when a person is emotional that you get to see their real nature. You get to see what they are really thinking and feeling. Bottling it all up is just going to make it harder. I might not have a solution, but I will always listen to what he has to say. I always reassure him that I won't judge him when he's in a bad place.

I think that's something that everyone needs to learn. It's not okay to judge people by their flaws. Is it so hard to look for the good in people? All judging is going to do is make the person feel bad about themselves and develop an inferiority complex. Do we really need that?

Through your actions, remind people that there is good in the world. Make them feel safe when they are showing you their vulnerable side. Make sure they feel validated and safe.

CHAPTER SIXTY-TWO

DON'T JUDGE

It is high time that we stopped judging one another. It has far-reaching effects and consequences that we don't stop to think about. People have to think twice before making assumptions about others. One simply does not have the right to judge others, to begin with. We shouldn't be so quick to judge without knowing the whole story. People don't take the time to understand the situation but are so quick to comment on things. I cannot emphasize that enough. We shouldn't judge without knowing the whole story.

To put it into practice, before you judge someone, take a moment to think about what they would feel. Try putting yourself in their shoes in that situation. If you can't understand what they are doing or why they are doing what they're doing, it doesn't mean we have the authority to talk behind their back. It just means that there are things that they want to keep private. Imagine if you were in a similar situation. Would you want people to spread trash about you? So it's better to keep one's opinions to oneself if one lacks the mental capacity to empathize with another person.

It is important to acknowledge the consequences of one's words and the power they hold against their victim. They would end up raising their inhibitions and making themselves defensive. This means the victim has to constantly look over their shoulder. They end up changing who they are, even when they did nothing wrong. Why? Just to stop someone from spreading rumors about them. They might be in a bad place mentally. They might not have the energy to defend themselves from the world. It's better to hold one's tongue than to make things harder for others. The worst part is that when a person spreads rumors about someone, more people tend to believe them. Eventually, they might believe that they are doing something wrong - when they are just being themselves. There's nothing wrong with being genuine. All they are getting in return for being honest about themselves is gossip and accusations behind their backs. Their self-esteem also crumbles in the process.

We all have to remember that our words have power. One can turn people against others. For what though? We might have a little grudge against them or there might have been a misunderstanding. But it is imperative to remember to treat them with respect. When even their comfort circles start treating them with hostility, where would they go? This may even lead to severe cases like depression or even worse - suicidal thoughts. It may seem insignificant to some but it definitely goes a long way.

Finally, I'd like to remind you that it's important to treat others with basic respect, no matter how much you may hate them or how much your ideologies may differ from theirs. Everyone is just trying to live their lives. The world doesn't need more toxicity. Don't add on to the flame and start tempering your tongue.

CHAPTER SIXTY-THREE

MAKING SOMEONE FEEL SPECIAL

People these days don't feel like they are special to their loved ones. They feel like they can be replaced easily and that they aren't really worth much. Everyone deserves to feel special. Right? These are some things that I do to make my loved ones feel special and things that I have noticed them doing for me.

The first one is listening to them. I don't mean tolerating what they are saying, I mean really listening to them. You have to show them that what they have to say really matters to you. When they think that they are replaceable, reassure them, saying that they can't be replaced. Remind them that you care. Remember, it's not just about words. Prove it to them through your actions. Spare time for them, even if it means rearranging your schedule. Make it a point to include them in your life. Show them that they are important to you. (This can even be as simple as asking for their opinions.) Make them feel needed. Have deep meaningful conversations with them. This shows that you value their opinions. Do things for them that you wouldn't do for anyone else. (To me, putting down my book for someone is a sign that they are special to me.)

You can also surprise your loved ones with things that they like. Things that they may have mentioned that they have been wanting for a long time. You can take them to places that they want to visit. Give them sincere compliments. Make it clear to them that you notice the little things about them, that many people probably overlook. Be sure to remind them that you will be around for them when they need support.

One of the ways that people make me feel special is by remembering little things that I have told them. They do things that I like even if they aren't totally involved in it. They take the time to know what I like and dislike, my fears, hopes, and dreams. They are a little possessive over me, which shows me that I am important to them. They constantly wash away my doubt and my negative thoughts while valuing my opinions. They cheer me up when I need to be.

Every person needs different things to make them feel special and loved. Learn what those are and make sure your loved ones know that they are very special to you.

CHAPTER SIXTY-FOUR

BLIND TRUST

Blind trust is so beautiful. It's literally putting your life into another person's hands and believing that they will take care of you. There are no strings attached. No doubts. No judgment. No fears. It's a sign of unconditional love. You trust that nothing will happen when you are with them. You can just close your eyes and jump off a (figurative) cliff and know that they will catch you.

You know that they have your back. You know that they won't judge you. Blind trust also promotes loyalty. I mean, think about it. You literally tell them everything about yourself. They know who you are, inside out. Would you do that if you didn't believe that the other person would be loyal? You trust that your secrets will be safe.

Blind trust also deepens a relationship. It leads to you being willing to share things with your friend or partner, which is important in any relationship. It encourages open communication. There aren't really many boundaries, just truth.

Personally, I have one person who I blindly place my trust in. I know that they (I am using a gender-neutral pronoun to protect their identity) are always going to have my back. They constantly tell me that when push comes to shove, they are going to be there for me. "It's us against the world," they promise. This person is my rock and my safe space. I feel safe trusting them with my secrets, knowing that they won't judge.

Isn't that what blind trust is? I consider myself really lucky to have them in my life. I'm sure I can handle anything with them by my side.

CHAPTER SIXTY-FIVE

ONE GOOD HUG

Close your eyes and imagine seeing your favorite person in front of you. This is the person you feel safest with. The person who knows you inside and out. Imagine them smiling at you and opening their arms wide. They nod at you and you break into a smile. You run to them and jump at just the right moment. You jump into their arms and they catch you. You wind your arms around their neck as they spin you around. You feel yourself melting into their embrace and sighing, all the worry inside you melting away.

Imagine sitting in the arms of someone you really love. Or sitting on their lap, their arms around you. Your head is resting on their shoulder or chest. You can feel their steady breathing. You can feel their hair tickling you. Imagine feeling time stop when you are there. Your breathing slows down and you calm down. The world slows down and your mind stops spinning.

That feels really good, doesn't it? One good hug is all you need. It can be the solution to all your problems. When we hug someone that we love, we feel complete. This is because their heart is on the side opposite to yours. It feels like both sides of your body have a heart, at that moment.

Let's look at it scientifically. A hug slows down our heart rates and decreases the level of the stress hormone in our body. Hugging makes us feel calm, safe, and relaxed. Hugs allow your body to release oxytocin, which relieves stress and promotes feelings of happiness or contentment. Hugging also releases endorphins, which are the body's natural painkillers. This is why a hug feels like it can physically heal you.

Emotionally, a hug makes you feel loved. You feel safe in the arms of someone you love. This builds trust and allows you to open up more. This leads to open communication and honesty. A hug also boosts your self-esteem. You must have heard of the phrase 'hug it out.' A hug can be the solution to misunderstandings or conflicts.

To me, a hug makes me feel validated. It makes me feel like I'm worth being loved. A hug makes me feel safe and comfortable around the other person.

Hugs are really important. Get out there and hug your loved ones!

CHAPTER SIXTY-SIX

Just Cry, It's Okay

"Just cry. It's okay," is something that people need to hear more often. People think that tears are a sign of seeking attention, being weak, or not being able to handle things on your own. In reality, I believe that tears are a sign that you have emotions. It means you are human.

People are so afraid of being judged that they just pretend that they are okay with whatever is thrown at them. They prefer to suffer alone while acting happy and cool in front of other people. People are scared that they will be ridiculed if they express their negative emotions.

I disagree with this and encourage people to express themselves. Bottling it all up is just going to hurt. Maybe even physically. It's just going to increase your anxiety and stress you out. Holding in all the hurt you are feeling will lead you to keep dwelling on the things causing negativity.

Crying is an emotional release for pent-up emotions. Even happiness. I think it's strange that tears of joy are encouraged and celebrated while tears of sorrow are judged. When people cry out of sadness, their problems aren't validated. People tell them that they aren't the only ones with problems. But, people deal with problems in different ways. Some people need to cry first. This clears their mind so they can think logically to solve their problems. Crying is normal and I think it's cruel that people are led to be scared to do so.

I think people need to hear that someone will let them cry. Someone needs to tell them that it's okay to cry their heart out and that they are there for them. Go be that person for someone. I'm sure they will be really thankful for you. Just reassure them that you won't judge. Remind them that they don't have to be ashamed of their feelings.

CHAPTER SIXTY-SEVEN

How To Say Goodbye

Is there any proven way to say goodbye to someone you love? I don't think so. I think the most important thing to remember is that if you really love someone, goodbyes aren't permanent. It's just 'goodbye for now.' You are telling them that you look forward to seeing them again.

Saying goodbye isn't easy, but sometimes, it's inevitable. I agree that it's really hard to say goodbye to someone who you have grown close to. It's heartbreaking to see them leave you behind. There's nothing you can do but let them go.

You have to remember that you'll still have their memories to keep you company. Those moments you shared will give you comfort in the days to come. You will miss them immensely. There's no way to get around that. The initial days will be the hardest. Everything you see will remind you of them. You won't be able to go anywhere without their absence engulfing you. Everything you do will scream emptiness. It will be raw and it will hurt. You might feel like something is eating at you from inside. Your heart and your entire physical being will ache to see them again. (Especially if you don't know when you will ever see them again.)

I don't think there is any way to get past this completely. I think it's all about knowing that they too will be thinking of you, somewhere far away. You believe that they miss you as much as you miss them. That is the only thing that will give you comfort.

CHAPTER SIXTY-EIGHT

SOUL MATES AREN'T SIMPLY ROMANTIC

I don't believe that a soul mate has to be romantic. I believe that a soul mate can be someone who you really connect with. Not just on an external level. I mean someone who you connect with in a way that seems to transcend earthly planes. A platonic soulmate is someone with whom you share a friendship that goes as deep as it can go.

I believe that platonic soul mates are as important as romantic soul mates. Yes. You can have both.

It is someone who you immediately connected with. By that, I mean that there wasn't a period where you felt uncomfortable with them. You both understand each other very well. There is no jealousy, no competition. When you met them, you might have regretted not meeting them earlier in life. They are really important to you. (And no, you don't feel anything romantic towards them. Yes. That is possible.)

You believe that there is no judgment. You feel safe sharing your secrets with them. The friendship is easy and supportive. You both want the best for the other. You are also genuine with each other. By that, I mean that you are your true self around each other. You don't feel the need to put on a mask.

I think that this is a relationship that everyone needs to have. You can have more than one platonic soulmate. It's pretty simple. It's just someone who you connect with more than others. The best part is that this relationship is easier than a romantic one. Even if you both don't talk for a while or are separated for a while, the relationship is still healthy. You feel good in their presence and they make you feel worthy and loved.

CHAPTER SIXTY-NINE

WHERE YOU BELONG

A sense of belongingness is something that everyone craves. It's a basic human desire. I'm talking about the sense of belonging that comes from a person. (I don't mean it only in the romantic sense.) The question is, how do you know when you have found that person?

Have you ever been with someone and felt like you just belonged there? They are your home and your safe space. You never doubted it. You don't have to be worried about being judged in their presence. It's just right. No competition. No fears whatsoever. Just comfort, trust, and affection. You know that your rightful place in the universe is by their side.

Now, what would you do when that person is gone? Suddenly, they aren't a part of your life anymore. When you look around, all you see is emptiness. Remember, this person was the only one who made you feel like you didn't have to hide. You felt seen in their presence. They made you feel important and valued. They gave you the assurance that they wouldn't judge and proved it over and over again.

There's nothing to do but to trust fate. If you truly belong by their side, you will remain there. No one else can take your place there. But, what would you do if they changed too? What if they prove that they are just like everyone else that you have encountered?

CHAPTER SEVENTY

The Maternal Instinct

I believe that a woman doesn't need to give birth to a child of her own to have maternal instincts. After all, motherhood isn't for everyone. Some women are terrified of having children of their own but have a very maternal nature.

I believe that maternal instincts develop in girls early on. Younger siblings are like children to them. As they say, older siblings grow up with their parents while younger siblings are raised by their older siblings. They develop due to nurturing relationships formed with others. It comes with a feeling of protectiveness, love, and concern.

It can also develop because of a woman's profession. If she is employed in a job where caring for others is essential, like teaching or nursing, she develops a maternal instinct naturally. These professions cultivate qualities like empathy, patience, compassion, and a nurturing spirit. Pets also evoke these instincts.

A mother is someone who is supposed to provide unconditional love, guidance, protection, care, etc. I think that anyone who has an abundance of these qualities has great maternal instincts. It's basically a tendency to protect others from harm. You want to envelop them in your arms and make sure that they are safe, loved, and cared for. You know when your 'child' is in danger and your first instinct is to save them and protect them from any further harm. Your touch is the only thing that can calm them down.

This also entails embracing your 'child' for who they are. It means unconditional love and the absence of judgment. You might even feel a maternal instinct developing when you are with your friends. You want them to grow and their successes bring you joy. Their failures bring you equal sorrow.

Now, think about it, who do you think cares for you like a mother (other than your biological mother)?

CHAPTER SEVENTY-ONE

Home Can Be A Person

What do you think home is supposed to be? Home is supposed to be a place you feel safe in. It should be a place where you can be yourself. You can have more than one home. You can have a home away from home. A house doesn't necessarily need to be a home. A house is just a building that you live in. But, the word 'home' means that there is some emotion attached to the building.

You can even find a home in a person. They give you the same feeling that a physical home does. They make you feel safe. When home is a person, you feel safe and secure, no matter where in the world you are. You could be miles away from where you grew up, but you feel cared for when you are with your 'home.'

I think it's one of the most beautiful things to make a person feel at home with you. It shows you how much a person trusts you. When someone calls you their home, it means that you give them peace of mind. You let them be themselves. They don't have to worry about facing judgment from you. They feel like the love they receive from you is totally pure.

I really believe that home can be another person. As long as that person makes you feel the same emotions that you associate with a physical home. Think about who your 'home' is and make sure you tell them how special they are to you. Make sure they know how much they mean to you.

CHAPTER SEVENTY-TWO

LOSING YOUR BEST FRIEND

When you lose your best friend, you feel like you lose a part of yourself. You find that everything reminds you of them. You are also reminded of the fact that they aren't around anymore. Everywhere you look, there's only emptiness.

Imagine your best friend. The one person who you could trust completely. You would quite literally put your life in their hands. You might not have known them for long, but the bonding that you share is inexplicable. They were your constant companion and were pretty much a ray of sunshine. You would turn to them if you needed anything at all. They were your source of inspiration and the only one who kept you going.

Now, think about this situation. You are the only one who has the time to miss your best friend. All you have is time and that hurts. It hurts so much you feel like tearing your heart out of your chest. You feel like it would be better to simply turn off all your emotions. You feel like a burden. You feel like you are clingy. You feel like you are seeking too much attention. Remember that this person is someone who you used to talk to about every single mundane thing.

But now, you find yourself wondering if they could spare the time to listen to you. Whether it's a simple laughing matter or a serious problem. You wonder if it would be distracting for them to have to listen to all you have to say. After all, you still do want the best for them and you don't want to be the reason for their loss of focus.

In the end, you end up thinking it's for the best if you internalize your emotions - positive or negative. You think it's better if you keep your stories to yourself. You feel like it might not be worth having hope anymore. You feel guilty when you ask them for something. You wonder if you are expecting too much. You wonder if you even have the right to hope or wish or expect. You wonder if you have the right to be mad or sad or just to miss them.

There is also a small part of you that wonders whether you mean as much to them as they do to you. That's a fear that you just can't shake. No matter how many times they may have reassured you in the past, you feel like you are never enough. And you feel like you aren't worth it. You wonder if they finally realized that and decided to move on.

The point I'm trying to make here is that when you lose something like that... even though it's involuntary, a piece of you dies with it. I'm not talking about simple friendships here. I'm talking about someone you share a deep emotional connection and understanding with. It's heartbreaking to imagine what your life would be like if they were gone. At this point, you don't even want to look for another friend. You are so scared that things might go in the same direction and you know you just can't take that pain again.

CHAPTER SEVENTY-THREE

HELP!

How do you help someone you love when they are in need? Is there any particular way that you can help? What if you aren't really sure what to say? This is a question that has stumped me for so long.

Imagine that someone you love needs you. You are the only person they talk to and they need your support. But, here you are, with no idea how to help. Some of the things they say might be completely new to you. The only thing you are sure of is that you aren't going to let them deal with things on their own. You know that your conscience wouldn't allow that. Be honest, would you be able to rest easy knowing that they are suffering - or are in any kind of pain?

Physical pain is easier to help with. You could go sit by their side, holding their hand and assuring them that they will be alright. But when it's emotional, you can often find yourself at a loss about what to do. Sometimes, there's no right thing to say. You just have to take extra care not to hurt them any more than they already are. You just have to assure them that you aren't going to leave them, no matter what happens. It might be hard sometimes. It might take a toll on you. It's going to demand a lot of your attention. But, if you really love them, it's worth it. Right?

You might not be able to help them, but the fact that you try to do so has to count for something. Just try your best. Give it what you have.

What would you do if something like this happened?

CHAPTER SEVENTY-FOUR

One Piece Of Jewellery

Have you ever had a piece of jewellery that was a huge part of your identity? You wore it so often that it became an irreplaceable part of you. (Yes, there could be more than one accessory.) There was some deep significance as to why you wore it. Maybe it was a gift from someone you loved. Maybe it was something that you and a friend both wore together. Maybe it was something that reminded you of an unforgettable incident in your life. Maybe it was something that made you stronger.

If someone gifts you that piece of jewellery, it can bring you comfort. By that, I mean that you crossed their mind for a moment. As soon as they saw it, they thought of you. It means that they care enough about you to get you that article - no matter how small it might be. The pleasure that you attain when you receive it doesn't disappear over time. It just grows every time you wear it. It feels like you have a part of your special person with you all the time.

The main point is that that piece of jewellery is part of who you are. People knew that you always wore that piece. If you didn't wear it, it meant that something was wrong.

What if you no longer want to wear it though? Obviously, you would have put a lot of thought into committing to wear it. Why would you want to stop all of a sudden?

The only reason could be that the article no longer means anything to you. Or, even worse, it might make you feel sad. If a relationship ended, you wouldn't want to wear something that was a symbol of what you once had. For a while, you are going to feel like something huge is missing. You unconsciously feel like the place it is supposed to be is empty (For example, you unconsciously rub your collarbone to feel your favourite pendant.)

It doesn't matter what it is or how expensive it is. All that matters is what it represents and how it makes you feel.

CHAPTER SEVENTY-FIVE

It's In The Little Things

It's the little things that matter more than anything that's materialistic. Materialistic gifts are nice to give and receive, but they don't come close to the little things. By little things, I mean the things that show you that you are important. Things that make you feel loved and appreciated.

Imagine how good you feel when someone takes the time to listen to you talk. They listen for hints of what you like and don't like. They take the time to get to know you. Those are some of the little things I'm talking about.

Another one is when a person makes time for you. No matter how busy they are, they make sure to spend some time with you. Or, they at least make sure to let you know that they are busy and that they will come to talk to you as soon as they can. They don't leave you waiting is what I mean to say.

They make you feel like a part of their life. Their future plans might include you - or rather, they include you in making big plans or decisions. They tell you about things that they did, no matter how trivial they seem.

The most important point to remember when it comes to the little things is whether or not the person receiving it will like it. These things are supposed to make them feel loved and appreciated.

CHAPTER SEVENTY-SIX

TRUE DIAMONDS

So, the inspiration for this post originated from a typo. My friend was telling me to try the song 'Diamonds.' When he typed it out, it said 'true diamonds' instead of 'try diamonds.' So, here it goes.

When I heard this, I started thinking about who a true diamond of a person was. A gem - or a diamond - of a person is obviously very rare. You might not find a person like that often. When you do, make sure you don't try to push them away or chase them away. You will regret it once you lose them and you might find yourself wishing you realised what you had when they were by your side.

We can also say that they are expensive. By that, I mean that the relationship takes a lot of effort to maintain, but it's surely worth every ounce of energy you spend. There are going to be times when you want to let go. You might find yourself doubting whether the relationship is worth it or not. But trust me when I say this, a good, strong, healthy relationship takes loads of effort. You will have to adapt yourself to suit the other person - and they will have to do the same for you. It's a sign of how strong your bond is when you don't complain about things you have to do for the other person.

LOVE IS A NEED

Here, I don't only mean that receiving love is a need. Giving love is also an equally important need. (Whether romantic or platonic.)

There are times when you absolutely need to receive love. There's nothing else that can cheer you up. All you want is to lie in the arms of your favourite person, doing nothing at all. You could be sitting in complete silence and it wouldn't matter. Or you might just want some acknowledgment. You might want them to remember your presence. You could be expecting something really small, like them remembering your favourite things, but you might not have the courage to ask them. Or rather, you might be curious to see if they would do it without a push from you.

Giving love is something that makes one feel needed. When you shower love on someone, you feel like you can do something useful. They make you feel needed - which, let's face it, really helps with one's self-esteem. If you are away from that person for a while, the need just intensifies. You can't help but shower them with all the love and affection that you have been holding back. It might feel like you are smothering them, but it's not something you can help.

The point I'm trying to make is that love isn't something that can be avoided, or put away to give or take at a later time - according to your convenience. It's just something that's totally natural and it doesn't conform to the boundaries of time.

CHAPTER SEVENTY-EIGHT

TURNING OFF YOUR EMOTIONS

Why do people assume that things can only get done if you do them without any emotion? I mean, doesn't having emotions make you better suited to make decisions. You can make good decisions if you feel passion for what you do. Isn't passion an emotion?

On the other hand, sometimes I have wondered whether it would be more convenient to turn them off. I have to admit that they get in the way sometimes. Also, emotions hurt. They can make you lose your mind and lose your cool. They might lead to divides in relationships - any kind of relationship. You might feel like you are being too clingy or that your affection isn't reciprocated. Without emotions, you can simply focus on your goals. You can drive all of your determination into what you have to achieve. But, again, what's the point in accomplishing anything if you can't be happy about it?

Losing your emotions can also protect you. It can protect you from getting hurt. It can help you make reasonable decisions. (I don't have a lot to say here because I don't think people should turn off their emotions, even though I am heading in that direction myself.)

I understand that I have been talking about two opposing arguments here. (I'll let you know when I pick a side.) But, the thing is, it's hard to pick a side. I admit that I still don't know if emotions are worth it. Positive emotions lead to getting yourself hurt. Negative emotions send you spiraling. There are some times when you can't be emotional, but what if those times occur so frequently that you forget that you are a human being capable of feeling emotions? You have to realize that you have every right to feel emotion. Yes, people will tell you otherwise. They will try to cut off your emotions. But, you can't lose them. Your emotions are what make you you.

(I wish I could hammer that into my head. I hope it helps someone though.)

CHAPTER SEVENTY-NINE

HANDMADE GIFTS

Why is it so special to receive or make handmade gifts? Why is it different from something store-bought and materialistic? Instead of some expensive present, imagine receiving something personal, like a handmade birthday card or a poem written on fancy paper. I certainly would prefer a handmade present.

When you make a handmade gift, you put your love in it. You invest plenty of time and effort in it. There's something that you add to it that you can't find anywhere else. You wouldn't be making someone something if you didn't know them well. That means that you know exactly what that person likes. You can be sure to add things that you know they will love. You can't go wrong.

When you receive one, it shows how special you are to someone else. You know that they value you in their life when you see that they took the time to make you something. You can feel the love they instilled in it. Whenever you look at it, you are reminded of them. You are reminded of all the good memories you have of them. You feel warm and cozy when you think of them.

I think handmade gifts are really precious. They are something to be cherished forever.

CHAPTER EIGHTY

YOU DIDN'T LET ME FEEL LONELY

The inspiration for this post actually comes from two of my professors. For the sake of their personal anonymity, let's call them Professor A and Professor B. Professor A was telling the class a story about Professor B's first day working in college. So, Professor B was waiting outside the department room while Professor A noticed that he had been standing there alone for quite a while. Professor A invited Professor B inside the room and offered to give him some company. Later, Professor B thanked Professor A for his company and said something along the lines of "You didn't let me feel lonely," in gratitude. (Please excuse me if I didn't quote the sentence exactly.)

When I heard this, I was reminded of a couple of people in my own life who have never let me feel alone. These people remind me that I don't have to do everything on my own. They make sure I don't get lost - metaphorically. These few people make things worthwhile.

I consider myself very lucky to have them. It's not just that they give me company during the day, there's more to it than that. They encourage and support me in my endeavors - my writing for instance. They push me to chase my goals. They celebrate my successes by my side while making sure that I know that they will stand by my side no matter what.

When my professor told the class this story, these are some of the thoughts that raced through my mind. I realized that no matter what I feel at the moment, I am never really alone in this huge, scary world.

CHAPTER EIGHTY-ONE

SETTING UP BOUNDARIES

A lot of people today have problems with setting up boundaries. They think that boundaries will make a person drift away or that it will spoil the relationship. In reality, boundaries are what define the relationship. People are afraid to say no and just go with the flow. This leads to internal conflict and might make the person feel unsafe.

It's okay to set different boundaries with different people, depending on how close you are to them. You can have different boundaries with your close friends than with your loved ones. If people can't accept the boundaries you set, it's best to distance yourself from them. You don't need to explain your motives. All that matters is that you feel emotionally and physically safe. They help build respect and trust.

People who are needy or co-dependent struggle with setting boundaries. They are scared that they will be left alone because of their boundaries or conditions. They are desperate for love, attention, and affection. They sacrifice their unique identities to achieve this. Boundaries are not a sign of insecurity. They show that you have a good sense of self-respect and dignity.

You want your boundaries to be respected. Right? Similarly, make sure you respect boundaries that other people set - even if they aren't the same as yours.

CHAPTER EIGHTY-TWO

DARK ROMANCE

These days, dark romance has become very popular. It has created a fan base for itself and has a lot of avid readers. It features tension between the main characters and the characters are very complex and flawed. It usually features one character who is openly dark – i.e., he or she doesn't try to hide it. The other character hides his or her dark impulses until he or she meets the other character, who makes him or her open up.

Dark romance has darker themes and is riddled with mature content. You should be aware of the content in the book before diving into it. There are morally grey characters and violent plots. The characters have faced a lot of traumatic incidents which made them 'the way they are.'

When you try to write a dark romance, there are some things that you need to keep in mind. For starters, the characters have to be built well. You need to show off their different layers and complex motives. You can shine a light on their inner demons and personal struggles. You can even give the audience glimpses of their past, making the character more understandable. The character has to be easy to hate and hard to love.

Make sure you decide on an appropriate setting and time. For example, a human trafficker can't meet the girl who changes him at a mall. A better place for them to meet would be a dark bar where the girl is looking to satisfy her dark impulses. Incidentally, this could be where the trafficker picks his victims.

You can feel free to dive deep into human emotions that might not be suitable in a conventional romance. These emotions can be confusing and utterly unwelcome. Also, make sure to invest time into a good plot. Don't just make your book about forbidden romance. Give it a purpose. Give it something that makes readers want to know what's going to happen next.

Examples of dark romance books are the 50 Shades series and the Twisted series.

Readers, beware when you dive into a dark romance. Make sure you know what you are signing up for. If you have some deep inner trauma, this may not be the genre for you. Writers, make sure to include a warning when you publish your work. You wouldn't want to hurt anyone.

Have fun!

CHAPTER EIGHTY-THREE

PRINCESS TREATMENT

Princess treatment can mean different things to different people. To most people, it means receiving expensive gifts, getting all your demands fulfilled, and receiving special treatment. It might mean paying for everything, being taken out every day, being driven around everywhere, and including a lot of material things.

Traditionally, princesses have been portrayed as very delicate people. They have a lot of people waiting on them hand and foot. All their demands are fulfilled immediately. No one dares question her orders. This is what most people think when they see the phrase 'princess treatment.'

In my opinion, princess treatment isn't materialistic. It's more personal. It's still derived from the treatment that a traditional princess receives, but it's more emotional and psychological. My definition of princess treatment is that people don't let you go to bed when you are upset. They make sure to check on you and make sure that you are emotionally stable. It means that they take time to talk to you and value your opinions. They make you feel emotionally safe in their presence. Everything, from the way they talk to you or touch you, is gentle and they treat you like you are a delicate flower. It means that they are patient, kind, and emotionally available. They make you feel loved and needed, without using anything materialistic.

WHO SAYS?

This post is about "Who Says" by Selena Gomez. This is one of the most motivational songs that I have heard. It's not my usual music (I'm a total Swiftie), but it makes me feel good about myself. The first lines read 'I wouldn't wanna be anybody else. You made me insecure, told me I wasn't good enough. But, who are you to judge.' Here, I feel like people have made her very insecure in the past. They all told her that she wasn't worth it. At one point she probably would have believed it. Finally, she realizes that people don't have the right to judge. She realizes that no one can bring her down.

Then she says, 'I'm sure you got some things you'd like to change about yourself. But when it comes to me, I wouldn't wanna be anybody else.' Here, she reminds us that everyone has self-doubts. Everyone has things about themselves that they want to change about themselves. Now, she is confident in herself and says that she wouldn't change anything about herself. She has regained her self-esteem. She says that there's no one she'd rather be than herself.

Then, when she says 'I'm no beauty queen. I'm just beautiful me,' she is telling us that everyone is beautiful in their own way. They don't have to win a beauty pageant to be considered beautiful. This is something that everyone has to hear. Today, beauty is standard. There are ways that you have to look to be considered beautiful. I agree with Selena when she says these lines. Beauty is based on individual tastes.

The next few lines read 'Who says you're not perfect? Who says you're not worth it? Who says you're the only one that's hurting? Trust me. That's the price of beauty.' Here, she's telling us that no one has the right to make us feel inferior. No one can without our consent. She also reminds us that everyone has problems. When she says that that's the price of beauty, I feel like she's telling us that nothing can be achieved without pain and struggle.

In her bridge, she is telling us that we can do anything that we set our minds to. She says that we are capable of achieving all of our dreams.

I really love Selena for giving us this song. At first glance, it seemed like a simple upbeat song. When I looked at the lyrics, I saw that Selena was really trying to give us something that we really needed. If you haven't heard this song yet, go check it out now.

CHAPTER EIGHTY-FIVE

MOMENTS

The inspiration for this post comes from the song '2002' by Anne Marie. 'I will always remember...' It talks about a moment in the narrator's life that she will never forget.

I'm sure we all have a moment like that. One that lives on vividly in our memories. You can remember all the details. Close your eyes right now. Take yourself back to that moment. Remember where it took place. Remember who was with you. Remember the main 'characters' in your memory. Recall what you saw. Recall how you felt. Remember the sounds and smells. Let all your senses take you back to that moment. Allow yourself to lose yourself in the moment.

How does that make you feel? Is it a good memory or a bad one? Regardless of how you feel, the memory is strong. It's something you can see with perfect clarity no matter how much time passes. Memories like that are important. They are core memories. They play a significant part in the make-up of your character. Even if the memory hurts you, don't try to forget it.

The point I want to make here is that every single moment and memory has an important role in making you who you are.

CHAPTER EIGHTY-SIX

PERFECT

What is the definition of perfection? Is anyone really perfect? So, this is how the dictionary defines the word perfect 'having all the required or desirable elements, qualities or characteristics; as good as it is possible to be.' I think that everyone has different definitions of perfection.

Some people think perfection lies in beauty. But, beauty is also subjective. People prefer different things. Other people think perfection lies in intelligence or some other personal characteristics that one might possess. But, you can't change who you are just because someone else wants you to.

I think perfection is overrated. It isn't possible to please everyone. You shouldn't aim to be perfect in someone else's eyes. You should aim to be perfect in your eyes (that of course depends on self-esteem). You should be able to be who you want to be. You should believe that you are perfect. People who really love you won't try to change you according to their definitions of perfection. They will admire the fact that you are firm in your standards. They'll love you for who you are. They will believe that you are perfect just the way you are.

An important thing to keep in mind is that you can't be perfect for everyone. You just have to know what your standards are and set them. You can't compromise your beliefs.

CHAPTER EIGHTY-SEVEN

A Thousand Years

Ohhh... This song takes my breath away. Yes, the lyrics are pretty basic and simple. The tune is simple as well. The part I love about this song is the emotion behind the words.

For those of you who aren't familiar with the song, it was written by Christina Perri. It was written for the movie 'Breaking Dawn,' which is part of the Twilight saga. The song became a symbol of the love between Edward and Bella. It talks about the fear of falling in love. It also talks about the joy of falling in love, or rather knowing you are loved.

Every word rings with emotion. Then, there's the James Arthur version. That one brings me to tears. Every time I hear it, my eyes dampen. The singer makes me feel like I'm experiencing the things that the song is talking about. The way that the singer's voice almost cracks makes me feel like my heart is breaking tenfold. Even the way the artist breathes contributes to the emotion of the song.

There is genuine fear in the voice of the artist. He's so scared to fall in love, but when he sees the object of his affection standing there alone, his doubts and worries fly away. He makes us feel like he really has waited over a century to meet this woman. (Like Edward did in the Twilight Saga.) He swears that he will still love her millennia later. The way he sings makes me feel like there's truth and vulnerability in his words. It makes me feel like every word he's singing is true.

This is one of the best songs I have heard, again, not because of the lyrics, but because of the emotion conveyed by the artists.

WHAT IS LOVE?

In the immortal words of Olaf, love is putting someone else's needs before yours. In technical terms, love is a set of emotions and behaviour characterized by intimacy, passion, and commitment. It also includes care, closeness, protectiveness, attraction, affection, and trust.

'You want a love that consumes you. You want passion and adventure, and even a little danger...' said Damon Salvatore. Everyone deserves love, but most people think they don't. Love is a necessity, not a desire. Unconditional love is something that everyone needs. A love without any expectations, without wanting you to change. Just simple and pure eternal love.

One very important thing to remember is that love doesn't need to be romantic. It can be platonic as well. In my opinion, platonic love is the purest form of love. Anything motivated by platonic love is sure to be pure. Love can mean different things to different people. Different people expect different things from their loved ones. In my opinion, love isn't a choice or decision. It's something that happens unconsciously.

Love changes you without your knowledge. You adapt yourself to better suit your loved ones. You unknowingly mimic their habits. 'Imitation is the sincerest form of flattery.' They help you become a better person. You would do anything for them. As Olaf said, you put their needs before yours.

CHAPTER EIGHTY-NINE

DEALING WITH DEPRESSION

Depression has become very common among today's youth and it is a serious problem that needs to be addressed. These days hearing the word depression has become part of daily life.

You might feel like recovery isn't worth it. You might feel like you don't have the strength needed to recover and that it would just be easier to give up. The first step you take could be something really small, like taking a walk or calling a friend. Recovery isn't easy, but it is in your control. You get to decide whether you want to recover or not. If you don't, you're going to end up paying the price.

You have to remember not to isolate yourself. You might not want company, but surrounding yourself with people you love makes you remember that life is worth living. It reminds you that there are people out there who do care about you. You might feel embarrassed to admit that you need help, but taking that step can prove to be a turning point. Isolation is just going to leave you alone with your thoughts. You need to get out of your head and reinstate yourself in the world. I can vouch for this. If it wasn't for the people around me, I wouldn't have been able to get out of my head. They helped me see things clearly again.

The worst thing to do is to think you can deal with everything on your own. Feel free to ask for help, whether it's from your loved ones or from a professional. I didn't really feel comfortable going to a professional when I needed help. Later, I realized that things would have been easier if I had.

You might feel more comfortable sitting around doing nothing all day, but that's just counterproductive. Distracting your mind is very useful. A couple of distractions I used were reading and art. Make sure you are always busy and don't allow yourself time to dwell on the past. Try learning something new or get back in touch with your favourite hobbies.

Don't give in to negative thoughts. Remember that things will get better. There's a whole world out there waiting for you to take it by surprise.

CHAPTER NINETY

ELDER DAUGHTER SYNDROME

Elder daughter syndrome can be explained as the unique pressures and responsibilities placed on the oldest daughter in the family. As an older daughter myself, I can assure you that this is true.

The eldest daughter has the most expectations placed on her, in the family. There is an extreme need to succeed and to prove herself. They have to achieve great heights and take care of their family. Yes, they learn independence early on, but with that comes guilt and shame.

There's a saying that goes something like this; "the oldest child grows up with the parents and the youngest child is raised by the older one." The firstborn children are like trials. The parents themselves are just figuring out what to do. They are young, too. There's something else that happens here. So, the older sister raises the younger one because their parents are still learning. But, when the parents do figure out how to raise the child, they reclaim them from the older sibling, who has spent most of their childhood taking care of the kid.

The elder daughter has to set a good example for her younger siblings. (I have a little sister and I find it very hard to be a good example for her.) It's not easy when one is a teenager themselves. They are just beginning to discover themselves, but they aren't given the space to do so.

Elder daughters feel guilty living their lives. They pretty much end up giving up their life for their family. (Yet, no matter how much they do, they are always constantly criticized.) They have to watch their parents grow up. They have to be good at everything and when something goes wrong, they feel like it's all their fault. They end up feeling like they failed and let everybody down. There is a lot riding on their shoulders.

I'm not saying that boys don't face this. I found it easier to write from a girl's point of view because this is something I go through. I'm sure older sons can relate to this post as well.

CHAPTER NINETY-ONE

WHAT'S THE POINT OF LOVE?

No really. What is the point of love? I'm sure I'm going to be philosophical, but this is a question that hit me a little while ago. Think about it. You love someone so much that it consumes you. A part of you knows that the relationship might not last. You can never shake that fear.

So, when you know this is inevitable (not many relationships survive these days), why do you fall in love? What do you get out of it? I think that love isn't a choice. It's something that just happens. You can't deny it. You can't decide to love someone or not to do so.

When you love someone, you give them the love that you think they deserve. This is actually really beautiful. Regardless of whether they reciprocate your love, your love is one of the biggest gifts you can give them. Obviously, you are going to think that they deserve everything you have to offer. You would be in their corner as their biggest supporter. You would be a great source of motivation. You would be the reason for their self-esteem to skyrocket. You might become the reason that they succeed. You make sure they realize their self-worth.

I think that the point of love is to make the object of your affection feel good. Love isn't supposed to be selfish. I know some of you might not agree with me here. But, when you truly love someone, you should make sure they feel prioritized. You should make sure that they know just how important they are to you.

I think loving someone isn't about you. It's about the person receiving your affection.

CHAPTER NINETY-TWO

WATCH YOUR WORDS

Your words have a lot of power. You have to make sure that you don't abuse them. You have to remember that the person you are talking to is also a person with feelings, just like yours. Be empathetic when you talk to someone. Before you speak, think of what you are saying. Once you say something, you can't take it back easily.

You have to remember that words can hurt a person more than something physical can. You have to be alert when you're talking. Your words might seem trivial to you, but they could have a really long-lasting effect on the person who receives them.

The person surely trusts you with their feelings. They hope you won't hurt them like they have been hurt in the past. But, think of how hurt they would be when you say something (obviously, you didn't mean it, but it still hurts.) That's when you have to be really careful. You might not be thinking straight. You might be caught up in the moment. But, that's not an excuse to say things without thinking them through. You might hurt someone you love. And I'm sure that's the last thing any of you want to do.

The point I'm trying to make is not to lose focus when you're talking to someone. Make sure you are fully aware of what you are saying so you don't regret it.

183

CHAPTER NINETY-THREE

ABUSIVE HOUSEHOLDS

What happens to a person raised in an abusive household? When I say abusive, I don't only mean it in a physical sense. Abuse can be mental or emotional too.

When a person grows up in such a household, small noises scare them. When they were young, a loud noise - or rather something banging around - meant that their parents were angry. Their flight or fight response is activated. They are instantly on alert. This sound was a sign that their parents might take out their anger on them. They have to be ready to defend themselves - physically or mentally. Even the sound of the door closing makes them jump.

When a person has been subject to emotional abuse, it means that they never feel like they are worthy. A small change in their loved ones makes them feel guilty. The change in the tone of how someone talks to them scares them into thinking that they did something wrong. They feel the need to apologize constantly because they know that they know that they can't bear to lose another person that they love. They might not have done anything wrong, but they still apologize. However, it takes them some time to realize that it's not their fault. After all, all they have known is that things are always their fault. Any small change in their parents' attitude was blamed on them.

Their parents blamed them for everything. Another sign is when a person has trouble displaying their emotions in public. In the past, they were criticized for showing any sort of emotion. If they laughed out loud, they were chastised for doing so. ("Why are you laughing over some nonsense? Are you crazy?") If they cried, they were accused of trying to guilt trip their parents ("Aren't we doing enough for you?" they would scream.)

They constantly have to question themselves as to what they did wrong. They are always wondering why their parents keep subjecting them to this. They never feel like they are enough and they can't believe it if someone assures them that they are indeed worthy.

If you see someone with these signs, be gentle with them. They are trying to get better. They are trying to get used to this kind of stuff, but you need to understand that it's hard. Home is supposed to be a place that nourishes a person and helps them grow positively. Think of how you would feel if you didn't feel safe in your own house.

CHAPTER NINETY-FOUR

You're Beautiful

I was listening to the song 'You Don't Know You're Beautiful' when I was inspired to write this. Everyone, please take a moment to listen to the song. When you do, imagine that the song is just for you. It's being sung for the sole purpose of making you realize that you are beautiful.

These days, there are 2 kinds of people. The first type is really vain about their beauty. The other type doesn't acknowledge that they are indeed beautiful. Let's look at the second type for now.

The song talks about a girl who doesn't know that she's beautiful even though there are signs all around her. For example, people stare at her when she walks into the room. She doesn't need makeup to look beautiful. She's perfect the way she is. But, it's obvious that she doesn't know that. Or rather, she doesn't feel beautiful. (No one has made her feel beautiful before.)

I think that everyone needs to know that they are beautiful in their own ways. Everyone is - in someone's eyes - the most beautiful person they know. You don't have to be beautiful in everyone's eyes. But, knowing that someone feels that way about you is magical and it really boosts your self-esteem. Everyone needs someone to tell them that they are beautiful.

Yes, this goes for guys as well. I know, most people think that the word 'beautiful' is associated with women only. I don't agree with that. I believe that men can be beautiful as well. There's nothing wrong in telling a man that he is beautiful. Try it out and see what happens.

CHAPTER NINETY-FIVE

IT ALL STARTS AT HOME

(Warning: This is pretty emotional and traumatizing. Read with care)

Everything you feel, good or bad, starts at home. Home is supposed to be the place where you feel safe. It should be somewhere that you can feel free to be yourself and express yourself. It should be where you can learn who you are. You should get support there. People at home are supposed to make you feel loved. But, what if you don't get these essential things?

What if your parents don't support the decisions that you make? (You are not a little kid anymore. You have ideas and dreams of your own.) Even if other people believe in you, there's always going to be a part of yourself that thinks you will fail because your own parents - who are supposed to know what you are capable of - don't think you will make it. What if your parents are the ones who tell you that you are fat (when you actually aren't)? You are going to end up starving yourself just to prove to them that you aren't.

What if they keep criticizing you at every turn? They don't have suggestions, but they won't let you try things out either. They call everything you do silly. They don't give you the space to learn about yourself. What if they don't allow you to show emotions (they scold you for shedding a tear or for laughing too loud)? You can't be happy or sad there. What would you do then?

This is why I believe that everything starts at home. Everything you like or dislike about yourself starts at home. Yes, happiness should come from within, but how will you be able to find that happiness without an environment that fosters love and peace? No matter how many times people tell you that you should love yourself, you won't be able to because the people who are supposed to love you unconditionally don't make you feel loved. You are going to end up feeling like you aren't worth being loved. I think that is the worst thing that you can feel. No matter how much love you receive outside your home, you are going to question it. Even if people assure you that their love is unconditional, you are going to wonder how someone can love you unconditionally.

That's when a home becomes a house. It is the worst feeling in the world when you can't feel safe and secure in the one place where you should be.

CHAPTER NINETY-SIX

SELF-HARM

Self-harm isn't just cutting yourself. It could be not looking both ways while crossing the road. It could be skipping meals. It could be not caring what you put in your body. It could be driving recklessly. What I'm trying to say is that self-harm isn't always explicitly visible. It could be as discreet as neglecting your needs, like sleep or food.

What we have to think about now is why someone would want to harm themselves. Obviously, they aren't going to tell you if you ask them. The worst part is that you can't always tell when someone is harming themselves. You can't see scars, or they might be hidden somewhere.

What can you do to help someone who has this habit (for lack of a better word)? Is there anything that can be done? Sometimes, people think that physical pain is better than mental or emotional pain. Or that it takes the edge off the pain that their mind is. No matter how much you tell them not to hurt themselves, they aren't going to listen to you. To them, all they want is a distraction from the pain their mind is in. They would give anything to turn it off.

The best you can do is try to help them deal with their emotions. They might feel like it's just too much to bear and they need an outlet. Even just listening to them, without judgment, could help them.

What I'm trying to say is that people don't harm themselves as a ploy for attention. They really need your help.

CHAPTER NINETY-SEVEN

SOCIAL ANXIETY

I was inspired to write this post when I heard a few of my seniors talking about social anxiety and how socially anxious people are often mistaken for introverts. I realized that not many people really understand what social anxiety is.

Social anxiety is an intense and persistent fear of being judged or watched by others. If it isn't dealt with, it can thwart a person's ability to form relationships. It can also keep them from initiating or maintaining a conversation. This anxiety can affect a person in all spheres of their life.

Social anxiety, which is actually mental, can also affect our body physically. People might feel nauseous in social situations. They might experience an increase in heartbeat, sweating, dizziness, blushing, stammering, or trembling.

People who have social anxiety dread how others think of them. They are very self-conscious and feel like they have a spotlight trained on them. They think that everyone is watching them, which makes them feel the need to be perfect i.e., they have high performance standards for themselves.

One way that a person can reduce their social anxiety is to build up their self-esteem. You are perfect. You just need to believe it. You don't have to worry about proving yourself to others. There are only a few people in your life who really matter, and if they genuinely care about you, they will love you for who you are. Another way is to practice public speaking. The more you do something you are afraid of, the easier it will become.

I believe that social anxiety can be overcome if you set your mind to it. You just need to be motivated properly.

CHAPTER NINETY-EIGHT

COMFORT

Comfort can be found in many different places. Your comfort zone is a place where you feel safe or at ease. What you find comfortable might not be comforting to someone else. (That's important when you are trying to comfort someone. You don't want to force someone into something that they dislike.)

Your source of comfort could be reading a book. It could be listening to music or playing a musical instrument. It could be working out. It could be binge-watching your favourite TV show or series of movies. It could be walking or just sitting alone. It could even be eating. It doesn't really matter what it is that brings you comfort. The only thing that matters is that after you enjoy your 'activity,' you feel relaxed and at peace, and that the effects last for a while.

Your comfort zone could also be a person. They could be your home away from home. You could feel totally safe by their side. You don't even have to be with them physically. You could be talking to them over the phone or simply texting. It doesn't matter. Again, the only thing that matters is the relief it brings you. The sense of lightness that you feel after a simple conversation with them.

After a long day at work, school, or college, comfort and relaxation is something that your body really needs. Don't deny yourself of that basic necessity. Take care of your body - physically and mentally. You will thank yourself for it later. Go find your comfort zone and make sure you take the time to go there every day.

CHAPTER NINETY-NINE

EXPECTATIONS

Can you really expect anything from someone else? Do you have the right to do so? Can you meet someone else's expectations? What do you do when someone expects something and you are so sure you can't deliver? You feel like you can never live up to what they ask of you - even though it's something that they really need.

Let's look at having expectations first. I think it depends on who you expect things from. You need to make sure that they are okay with you placing expectations on them. I, however, hate expecting things from anyone. In the past, everyone I have expected things from - no matter how simple - has let me down. A part of me just shies away from depending on anyone for anything. I only ask for things if I absolutely need them. But, in the end, it's not a surprise to me if I am disappointed. The main idea is not to expect too much. If you do, you are just setting yourself up to be hurt. Ask yourself if it's worth it. If it is and if you truly believe that your hopes will be met, go for it. But make sure to think it through time and time again.

Then comes meeting expectations. I don't think you can live up to what someone wants from you unless you really want to. You can't just set your mind to doing it. It won't work. It has to be subconscious. Another thing to consider is that you just might not be able to do it. By that, I mean that you might want to, but you are literally incapable of doing so. What happens then? You have to admit that you have your limits. If the other person has genuine affection or even respect for you, they will understand. You shouldn't have to push yourself past your limits to do something, just because someone else asked for it.

I know, sometimes you might feel like you have no right to expect things from anyone, but take a moment and reverse the situation. You would want your loved ones to ask you for things. After all, we are all human. We all have needs. The important thing is how you ask and whom you believe.

THE BEAUTY IN SILENCE

Before I wrote this entry, I spent a very memorable afternoon mostly in silence. I'm someone who enjoys hearing people talking. I like to listen to what people have to say.

That afternoon, however, I experienced a lot of beautiful things in silence. I realized that silence was beautiful. Silence gives way to many beautiful experiences. There are things that really can't be expressed in words. As they say, actions speak louder than words, and actions are most profound in silence, without words to draw attention away from them. Affection, for example, can't always be expressed in words. A hug can mean more than a verbal declaration of love or care.

On the flip side, silence can also express negative emotions. Silence can express displeasure. If someone is quiet, we assume that they are upset. If someone doesn't talk to us, we assume that they are displeased with us. Silence is quite powerful.

Silence also is a tool through which we can find inner peace. We can take advantage of the silence and take the time to listen to our thoughts. It gives us time to think about ourselves. It lets us distance ourselves from the commotion of the outside world.

I think that some quiet time with someone helps strengthen or deepen interpersonal relationships. That's a good way to summarize the magnificent afternoon I had.

(I know I was a bit more formal in my writing than I usually am, but I didn't know how else to express this.)

SILENCE IS THE ULTIMATE SIGN OF TRUST

My inspiration for this entry came from the lecture I listened to first thing in the morning. We were talking about the essay 'The Eloquent Sounds of Silence,' by Pico Iyer.

He says "Silence, then, could be said to be the ultimate province of trust: it is the place where we trust ourselves to be alone; where we trust others to understand things we do not say..."

The meaning that we derived from this was pretty intense and deep. My professor claimed that a true relationship doesn't need idle chitchat. A relationship where two individuals really trust each other completely doesn't have idle chitchat. They have serious sit-down discussions but they don't feel a need to always talk to one another. On the other hand, individuals who don't fully trust their partner feel the need to constantly keep up a conversation. She gave us an example of a husband and wife. She talked about how the couple don't sit around talking all day - maybe in the initial days of their marriage... but not years later.

As I thought about this, I realized that it was true. If you truly trust someone, why are you going to constantly ask them about what they are doing? Yes, when you care for someone, you will want to know how their day went and you will listen to their stories attentively. The idle chitchat that I'm referring to is that which is spawned out of doubt and possessiveness. Sometimes, the reason you ask someone what they were doing is that they weren't with you and they weren't responding to your calls or messages. The absence of this 'noise' is the silence which the essay talked about. This silence is the sign of ultimate trust.

HANDS OFF: A TRUE STORY

I was inspired to write this post by something that happened to me. I was traveling to Pallavaram by train. There were no seats, so my companions and I were standing. I was clinging on to my big brother's arm. The train lurched to a stop at one of the stations. I was horrified to feel a strange touch on my lower back. I instantly realized it was an unfamiliar man's touch. I recoiled instinctively. Unfortunately, I'm naturally clumsy. I fell into my friend's arms. She asked me what happened. I was too disgusted to even speak coherently.

This touch wasn't accidental. The train was at a standstill and there was space behind me. He didn't need to touch me to get off the train. Out of the corner of my eye, I could tell that he wasn't a boy or even a young adult. He was a man older than my dad. That made the incident even more repulsive. I still have chills and shudders running up my body.

This has been normalized in today's society. A woman being touched by a stranger has become normal and isn't really taken seriously. In my opinion, it is a really serious issue. I couldn't even reprimand the man out of shock at what happened. It disturbed me so much that I stayed encircled in my brother's arms on the way home.

A woman should be able to travel safely. She shouldn't have to keep looking over her shoulder for some creepy guy. (No offense to the gentlemen reading this.) As they say, "It's not all men, but it's always a man," who a woman has to fear.

I'm sure most of you would be asking me why I wasn't in the ladies' compartment. I was with my brother. I should be able to travel with my brother without worrying about this stuff. Right? Other people might be questioning my wardrobe choices. For your information, I was decently and modestly dressed.

This has to stop. We, as the future of the country, have to be better.

THE GHILLI CRAZE

The movie 'Ghilli' was re-released shortly before I wrote this entry. I only got the opportunity to watch it weeks after the re-release. At first, I wanted to watch it to know what all the fuss was about. (I admit, I had my doubts about it. I only watched the movie once before and I barely remembered what the story was.)

Once the movie began, all my doubts flew away. The movie theatre wasn't full, but the energy that the movie's fans emanated was magnificent. It began as the first notes of music played. I could almost feel the anticipation rising among the viewers. As the hero, Vijay, appeared on the screen, the theatre pretty much exploded with cheers and claps and whistles. The same happened with the appearances of the heroine, Trisha, and the villain, Prakash Raj. I honestly didn't expect such an uproar in honour of anyone but the hero.

The audience quoted dialogues from the movie in sync with the actors on screen. The most iconic dialogue was, of course, Vijay's opening punch line, "Intha area, Antha area, Intha edam, Antha edam, all arealeyum aiya ghilli da."

One of the most memorable ones was "Chellam, I love you chellam." (The entire theatre called it out.) Another one that I loved, (it looked really innocent when the heroine said it) "Kaarapodi sapadnum pola irruku."

Another thing I really liked was the fact that everyone knew what was going to happen next. I know, it might seem unusual, but I liked it because of the laughter that erupted. Usually, it's considered proper etiquette to remain silent in the theatre, but that wasn't the case here. People were very free with their laughter. No one had to worry that they were laughing too loud.

Then came the dancing. No one could resist dancing to the movie's hit songs. I had expected this but it was still exhilarating to watch. (And to take part in.) People were rushing by me as they went to the front of the theatre to dance to the songs. The astonishing part was that they had the dance moves memorized. I couldn't resist joining in (no, I didn't have the steps memorized.)

By the end of the movie, I was sold. The craze about it was justified.

THE PERFECT DRESS

One day, I was out with my friends. I dragged them to accompany me as I tried on a bunch of dresses. I was having loads of fun. That's when I saw it.

It was so beautiful on the rack. It was black and simple. It was plain. There was nothing very special about it. Yet, it sang out to me. I had to try it on. I went to wait in line in the dressing room. When I put it on, I gasped. I didn't think I could look so good.

It was honestly the best thing I had ever worn. It stuck to my figure perfectly. As I turned around to get a better look, I found myself loving it even more. It felt empowering and powerful. Then, I looked down at my legs. (The dress was short. It didn't even come up to my knees.) I don't usually wear short clothes outside. I was a bit shy at first. I steeled up my courage. I assured myself that I looked amazing. I called my friend to come outside the dressing room and I scurried out to show it off. (I use the word scurried because that's literally what I did.) I felt like the dress was made for me. It was simply magnificent.

SEXIST JEANS

One of the major complaints that girls or women give for jeans is the size of pockets. It's something that I face as well. The pockets of my jeans are tiny. They barely even fit my phone. The back pockets are slightly bigger, but they aren't really safe.

Recently, I heard about the reason for this. Or at least what people think is the reason. So, traditionally men were breadwinners in the family. It was believed that they would have more money in their wallet - which goes into their pocket. It was believed that women wouldn't really have much money. This was the sexist thought that led to tiny pockets on pants and no pockets on most dresses.

Another reason for this might be to boost the sales of purses. If women had spacious pockets, they wouldn't need handbags.

Truth be told, women have more things to carry - other than their wallets. Our pockets can't even fit a sanitary pad. A lot of women even carry makeup with them. They don't fit in their pockets and women have to carry them in their hands.

Maybe in the past, small pockets could have been feasible. But now - in current times, it's not. Women's clothes need pockets. A handbag is cumbersome to carry around in my opinion. It could be used as an accessory occasionally, but when you don't have pockets, a handbag becomes a burden.

CANDY

This post is a tribute to my favourite stuffed animal. Yes, I know that's unconventional. She is a brown and white beagle. I have had her since I was around 2 or 3 years old. I eventually decided to name her 'Candy,' because I claimed she smelled like chocolates - I assure you, she doesn't anymore. She smells like laundry detergent after the number of times my mom put her in the washing machine.

A little while ago I had to go through something that I was afraid of. I remember how I used to take my stuffed animal to the doctor when I was younger. I started to recall all the memories I had with her.

She and I were inseparable. There is one moment that lives in my head vividly. One afternoon when I was around 7 or 8 years old, Candy went to take a bath - ie, she needed to be washed. I was waiting eagerly for her to come out of the dryer. When my dad opened the machine, I peered in and she was sitting on one of the 'wings' (I don't know exactly what they are called) inside the machine. 'She was waiting for you to find her,' my dad claimed. I pulled her out and cuddled her against my cheek, enjoying her warmth.

She would keep my nightmares away when I held her close as I slept. When I woke up scared, the first thing I would look for was her. I remember how I would tuck her into my bed, under the blankets, when I went to school. I remember rushing home to check if she was still there when I got back.

I just want to take a moment to appreciate how important a stuffed animal can be in a person's life. Especially one that has 'grown up' with them. There are a million more things I could say about Candy, but it would be best if they remained between the two of us.

WOMEN IN 18TH CENTURY ENGLAND

Dearest gentle reader,

The series, Bridgerton, is set during the glowing reign of Queen Charlotte, spanning between 1761 and 1818. Let us now look deeper into the state of womanhood during the time, which was often cloaked in silence and submission.

First and foremost, let us speak of feminism—a term rarely whispered and even more seldom embraced. Those who dared to speak of women's rights were scorned and maybe even cast away from society. Their words were paid no heed.

Women were revered as symbols of purity, their virtue guarded with extreme fervor. The mere thought of a woman meeting a man without the vigilant eye of a chaperone—be it a mother or a trusted female servant—was enough to spark whispers of scandal and ruin. In such unfortunate events, it was the lady's name and future prospects that bore the brunt of society's scorn. The man, however, would get off with no more than a reprimanding.

Those young ladies were brought into this world with a singular purpose: to marry. The destiny of every young woman was to leave the nest of her childhood and marry into another family, thus perpetuating the lineage of the family she married into. The choices she had in this matter were a luxury few could afford. Those who failed to secure a suitable match were often resigned to wed whomever their parents deemed fit, regardless of the suitor's age or appeal.

Women's education wasn't given much importance. Our young ladies were tutored in the arts that would make them desirable brides and competent mistresses of their households—nothing more. They were clueless about the outside world. Their protection passed from their fathers onto their husbands before they had a chance to blossom and explore the mysterious world around them.

(Yes, I tried writing this like Lady Whistledown would. I'm not sure if I achieved that goal or not. But I hope you enjoyed it. I'm sure that there are some aspects that I forgot about. These are all I could think of off the top of my head.)

KEEPING PROMISES

So, here's the thing. When you tell someone that you are going to do something, they end up counting on you. They might be someone who hates expecting anything from anyone. But, they can't help but believe you when you promise something to them. It could be really petty, or serious. In that moment, they trust you, whether they want to or not.

Now, imagine that the thing you promised them is something really important to the other person. It was something that they were really counting on. In the end, you end up breaking your promise. Imagine that this is a really personal situation. You were the only person they needed.

Think of the pain they would be going through. As I said before, they don't trust easily. But, they chose to trust you. They hoped that you would bring them relief. But, you couldn't. You couldn't keep your promise. You were their last hope. Now, all that's left for them to do is disappear. They were really hoping that you would be able to help them. Yes, it is a lot to put on someone's shoulders but take a moment to think of how highly they regard you if they were willing to all of their trust in you.

This is why I think it's really important to keep the promises that you make. You don't know just how much the other person needs it. You might be the only one who can help them. And you don't know what could happen to them if they are let down. The point I'm trying to make is to think about what you do or say. They have far-reaching consequences.

A GIRL'S GIRL

What does it mean to be a girl's girl? It's actually pretty simple.

I think it's really beautiful to be a girl's girl. It's really important for women to support one another. It's all about a woman being kind or genuinely good to another woman. She is a girl who respects other women and who knows how to treat them. One of the main things to keep in mind here is to respect the girl code.

This trend can be put in contrast to the 'pick me girl.' A pick-me girl does everything in her power to push other women down in order to get herself to the top. She is selfish and is willing to sabotage others. She is easily jealous and covets things that other women have worked hard for.

A girl's girl, on the other hand, celebrates other women. She feels genuine happiness for her friends. She would do anything to help a girl in dire need of assistance, even though she might be her greatest enemy. She might harbor some enmity, but she would help the girl if it was serious. She is honest and gives useful criticism. After all, no one can be right all the time. This is a way that women can get trustworthy feedback. A girl's girl doesn't feel jealous. She celebrates other women's successes. Back in the day, women were very competitive. For example, look at the portrayal of Regency England in Bridgerton. Young women had to compete with each other to secure a husband. They were made to rival each other.

A girl's girl doesn't have to swear off men. She doesn't need to restrict herself to female friendships alone. The important thing is that she never puts another woman down, just to be with her male companions.

It's all about embracing female companionship. The beauty that a woman feels when she is surrounded by a group of supportive and loving girls is like no other. It energizes and motivates her.

GIRL CODE

The most important rule in the 'girl code' is to rescue any girl who looks like she needs help. She might be your worst enemy, but you should never leave her alone in an unsafe situation. If she asks for help or signals you for assistance, you must help her.

The next one is to be honest. If a girl asks you how she looks or if something needs fixing, it's your duty and responsibility to be honest. You have to tell her if she needs to adjust her clothes or if she is too showy. (It's up to her whether or not she listens to what you have to say. You just have to make sure someone tells her. You never know if she is clueless or just attention-seeking.)

Then there is the basic rule about relationships. Girls, don't try to get with your friend's ex. Siblings are out of the question too (unless you have permission). Think about how the situation would make your friend feel. You don't want to have to choose between her and the object of your affection. That certainly would be an awkward situation. You can't let a guy get between you and your friend.

There are some things that you just shouldn't do. You shouldn't gossip about a girl behind her back. You should know the effects that unwanted or false gossip and rumors can have on someone. (This is even worse if you don't know the girl. What gives you the right to talk about anyone behind your back, especially when you don't know them?) Don't try to sabotage your friend. She probably trusts you a great deal. Think to yourself about whether it's worth it to break that trust she places on you. Respect her decisions, but make sure to correct them if she is wrong. Don't let her hurt herself. Don't ever tease or ridicule another woman. Again, you know how it would feel if someone talked down to you about how you looked or how you dressed.

Most of these are unspoken rules, but I think we need a reminder. It's a harsh world out there and we need to have each other's backs. (I didn't talk about periods because I think that's something really basic and there's no way you can ignore that.)

A Sneak Peek Into A Girl's Mind

(Disclaimer: This isn't universal. This is my point of view and many girls might have similar ideas.)

What are some of the things that go on in a girl's mind? I'm sure all of you guys are curious.

The first one is about how they feel when they go out. For some girls, going out is a treat and a rarity. They aren't allowed to do so often. So, when they do, they make the most out of the opportunity. Then, there is the conflict of what to wear when they go out. It's different depending on who they are with. If they are going out with their parents, the clothes they wear would be different from something they would pick to wear with their friends. They also have to make sure that the outfit they choose is appropriate for their mode of transport and their destination.

Guys, you might think girls dress for your eyes. But, that is not true. They dress up for themselves. They dress up to admire themselves in the mirrors. (Yes, that does seem a little self-centered.) They dress up according to their menstrual cycle and their self-care schedules.

I'm sure a lot of you might have asked yourself what a girl wants in a relationship - not necessarily romantic. In my opinion, the first and most important thing is safety. In today's world, safety has become a really big concern. When a girl hangs out with a guy, the first question she asks herself is whether she can trust him or not. Attention and other things come later.

Another thing that I have noticed is that people tend to think all girls are materialistic. They think that they need to receive gifts to be happy. It might be true in some cases, but not all. Simple things are important. Just take the time to show her that you care about her. Show her that you remember what she likes. Make an effort to make plans to hang out with her. Don't let her do all the work. Take some time to talk to her. She just wants to be loved. She doesn't need your money. She just needs you.

A woman will never admit that she needs help. She will try to project herself as being very capable and strong. Yes. She surely is. But, that doesn't mean that she doesn't love to be pampered. She's not going to ask for it. But, pamper her sometimes. Watch how her expression changes. Watch as she relaxes herself and forgets all her problems.

In contrast to the previous paragraph, a woman doesn't need protection. She is capable of taking care of herself. You don't need to be her knight in shining armour. Wait to see how she handles things. Only intervene when she asks you to do so.

Yes, I'm sure there are a whole bunch of things I missed. These are just some things off the top of my head. I'll try to give you some more when I think of them.

Comments

Remember that you are a woman

Anderlin

We mustn't lose sight of ourselves in this chaotic world. Not having a companion with you who understands and cheers you in your silent battles can be mind-numbing. Truly an eye-opening take on this!

Why does a girl need a brother in her life?

Anderlin

Love you too sis! Remember to never stop spreading your love across the world because the world needs kind people like you. I'll never stop being by your side. Again; my sis and me against the world.

Why does a woman need a male best friend?

Anderlin

Having a male companion is one of the most cherishing gifts ever. They push you to become a better version of yourself. (No offense to female companionship though)

Why is reading important?

Anderlin

Sounds reassuring. Definitely motivates one to get into the habit of reading

Christopher

As an avid reader of my own I do realize why books play a role in shaping individuals and how it is a leisurely activity where we don't have to use phones as a means to read something when you already got the stuff in your hands. Good work.

The Means to attain a happy life

Anderlin

If thinking that happiness is the only goal in life, we eventually become hedonistic. I believe putting ourselves through the trails of today to reap a better reward is a better way of living. Rather than giving into materialistic needs, we can focus on what we have and be grateful for the things we have. I believe that that's true happiness.

Damon Salvatore: Hero or Villain

Anderlin

Sounds like Damon turns out to be a hero huh? Well I should've known I guess. In my opinion villains always stand out to me because I believe villains are just heroes whose stories remain unspoken.

What is Back to December trying to tell us?

Anderlin

That's so sweet. Gotta give it to Taylor, her poetry is touching people's hearts and I think she is aware of her musical prowess.

'Speak Now,' said Taylor

Anderlin

Taylor does indeed is a good human for putting herself in her friend's shoes and empathising with how she would've felt. Letting a loved one go for another must surely be an unimaginable pain.

Mnemosyne 2024

Anderlin

Congratulations to us for conducting that event. We had so much fun together. I'm glad you and I were the ones to convene and judge the participants for this event. And for a fresher to do this much work... I'm proud of you.

The Faces People Wear

Anderlin

Only people close to us deserve our true selves. Other people just deserve the normal mask we wear around public. It is a relief to know that one can be whoever they want to be in their small but genuine circle.

Does Elena play the victim card too much?

Anderlin

That was quite 'on the nose'. I didn't expect to see a critical perspective that persuades people to see through the recurring misfortunes in a character because of the repetitive writing style. Good on you

A tribute to my seniors

Anderlin

This.... I'm officially breaking character for this one. This one is too heart melting that I can't write this without breaking character. Thank you Lekhaa for being one of the best juniors ever. I only hope that you pass on what you've learnt from your seniors onto your juniors.

Harish

Is someone cutting the onions. No. I'm really emotional.. with happy tears with memorable moments I spent with you lekhaa .. you're the best junior I ever had.. and I'm proud to be. How you are rising... Lots of love.

Shane

Okay u made me emotional. Thank you so much.

Sharan

Well well gonna miss this kid for real.

Embracing yourself

Anderlin

Well said. No matter what endeavour you are willing to undertake in life, you are bound to come across criticism. Rather than focusing on the criticism it is better to focus on ourself and be the best version of ourselves.

Princess treatment

Anderlin

Is this treatment only limited to princesses??? I'd love to normalise prince treatment.

Hands off: A true story

Anderlin

Sad that women have to constantly look over their shoulder in this society. I'm glad you got out safe.

Social Anxiety

Anderlin

Really bold of you to discuss about a topic which is so sensitive to people who undergo social anxiety. It needs to be discussed further so that people can find ways to overcome their fears of being judged. Great perspective!

Dealing with depression

Anderlin

My biggest pet peeves is when someone mistakes depression for laziness. Like dude... I don't even have the energy to get out of bed. Really hurts when they could just term it to a simple label like "lazy" when its actually more complex than that.

Sexist Jeans

Anderlin

This is so true. This is such a backward thinking for designing Women's jeans. This MUST be changed.

It's okay to be vulnerable

Anderlin

The harsh reality that some people feel is that they don't even know what's bothering them. They don't know what they're feeling or what it is that's bothering them. Maybe some people just find it hard to put their feelings into words because they don't even know why they're feeling what they feel in the first place.

Blind trust

Anderlin

I admire your blind trust. I could never place this level of trust on anyone. Maybe it's because of past traumas, but I hope I could trust people as much as you trust your friend one day.

Don't judge

Anderlin

Definitely an eye-opening essay. The world definitely needs less toxic people. And to people who say "respect has to be earned" should learn to treat others with basic levels of respect that they'd show to a stranger whom they don't know what they might be going through. An inspirational write up indeed!

One good hug

Anderlin

Some say it's just a hug, while only people deprived of those hugs truly value the soul connection that happens when hugging the person you love.

Making someone feel special

Anderlin

An endearing thought. This is how people should actually maintain relationships. Everyone must learn from this and keep a healthy relationship with their loved ones.

Just say "I loved you the way that you were"

Anderlin

"If someone can't stick around to learn why, did they even love you to begin with?" Facts!!!

How much sad did you think I had

Anderlin

It takes a lot of courage to just spit out what a person might be going through. It helps them a lot when someone they love gives them constant reassurance which helps them keep it together.

Soul mates aren't simply romantic

Anderlin

"You're The Kind Of Friend I Could Not See For Years, Not Really Talk To, And Just... Pick Up Right Where We Left Off." Words to live by...

How to say goodbye

Anderlin

If you believe that they loved you as much as you did, you can always assure yourself that they will remember you as long as you let them. That's what I believe atleast.

Elder daughter syndrome

Anderlin

This is true and I've seen it through countless others like in my cousin's family and my friends mostly. I feel like they shoulder an unbearable weight which they must carry out for their entire lives. I am the younger sibling and I think this goes on in every household as well.

It all starts at home

Anderlin

Home is a place of agency. When you are deprived of basic acknowledgment where you should basically get it from, it starts breeding the question, "Am I good enough?" among children. It kinds starts building up an impostor syndrome in you that makes you self-sabotaging and self-destructive.

Where you belong

Anderlin

Home is where the heart is. If you can't recognise that place anymore, it's no longer home.

What's the point of love?

Anderlin

I think when you love someone, you naturally start expecting things from them. Of course, true love is supposed to be unconditional but, what if they aren't given the attention or affection they deserve? You naturally start expecting things from them.

The maternal instinct

Anderlin

For me, my best friend who's now like a sister to me takes good care of me like a mother does. I'm very happy that I have her in my life.

You don't get to tell me about sad

Anderlin

That's a really valid point. No one knows what the other person is going through. So this gives us even more reason to be kind to one another since we don't really know what the other person is going through.

Last kiss

Anderlin

"The best way to love someone is letting them go," words to live by.

The Ghilli craze

Anderlin

Me and my sister went to this movie and we saw this little guy coming to our row and called my sister by tapping her with his tiny hands. It was an adorable gesture.

Perfect

Anderlin

No human being can ever be perfect. To be perfect is to conform to all the ideas of the other person and as we all know, not everyone agrees with the same ideologies as the other person. So it becomes paradoxical when someone is said to be perfect.

Am I allowed to cry?

Anderlin

Like I always say, the world needs less shitty people. We should start making a difference. Atleast the next generation of people should be less toxic

Kill the one you love

Anderlin

"I failed you as a lover, not because I wasn't good enough, but because I failed to show you just how much I love you."

'Cause he really knows me

Anderlin

My sister wears my initial on her necklace all the time. That must mean I'm winning as her brother!

Abusive households

Anderlin

As far as I've heard of abusive households, I could only tell that I couldn't last a day in one. I feel very sorry for people of the same age as me coming from an abusive household. It definitely breaks one, just to hear their stories. Imagine the person's feelings and how they must be tormented.

He who must not be named

Anderlin

This reminds me of a certain moment in the novel, Home, when the protagonist held his sister tightly while she was shivering to carry over her fears onto himself to hopefully stop her from shaking and not get spotted by their enemies. I was reminded of how beautiful brotherhood is. Very nice article!

Let it once be me

Anderlin

This reminds me of the character Allison from the movie, "Meet Joe Black". She constantly seeks her father's approval in the movie but her father doesn't care much. There is a particular scene where her father asks why she loves and does so much for him while knowing he doesn't care that much as she cares for his other daughter Susan. But Allison says that she feels loved and is always thankful for her father for providing for her. She knows she's not his favourite but she let's him know that it won't stop her from loving him with all her heart. Such an emotional scene.

HELP!

Anderlin

The fact that you feel bad and try to help as much as you want to although you don't have the answer to their worries shows just how considerate you are to that person. If they're a thankful friend, they'll definitely keep in mind those who never left their side when they are at their lowest.

Handmade gifts

Anderlin

One of the best things about handmade gifts is that it'll stay with you as long as you treasure it. This way you can keep collecting precious memories and cherish them for as long as you live.

Love is a need

Anderlin

An excellent take. I completely agree with you on this. Knowing your potential for love and not having that love to give can break someone. But they fail to realise that they need to accept that for themselves sometimes. You can't just be heartless and keep all your love locked away.

Teenage love taught you there's good in goodbye

Anderlin

Reminded me of another song by The Script called, "No Good in Goodbye". The lyrics are just ethereal and talks about a lover's unacceptance for losing his love and how lonely and hurting he is. He wishes to change all the things he did in the past to just somehow save his relationship. Just paints a wonderful picture about the pureness and the dangers of love.

True Diamonds

Anderlin

Learning to love someone can be hard but it is the only sign that shows that you truly love and care for that person.

Self-harm

Anderlin

Some don't realise that the other person is hurting until it's too late. People need to reach out to the person who is hurting even if they don't show signs of distress since we don't know what they might be going through. Because the last thing they want to do is reach out. Take care of your friends.

That line

Anderlin

Idk why but this Loki quote just popped into my head after reading this: "Sure. Burn it down, easy. Annihilating it, easy. Razing things to the ground is easy. Trying to fix what's broken is hard. Hope is hard." I feel like relationships are meant to be complicated and it's only a complete relationship when you learn how to love the person beyond all their imperfections. Having a bit of hope in your love would definitely get you farther in the relationship.

The very first night

Anderlin

The first days of staying apart from your loved ones is truly frustrating. During the first few months of getting into a relationship, livers can't stay away from eachother. They always want eachother's company and want to be inseperable. I love how the narrator sheds some light on some of my favourite parts of a newly developed romance.

Fearless

Anderlin

To leave everything you hold dear just to stand by your significant other to prove your loyalty may sound hardcore in fairytales. But as much as it sounds cool, it's toxic to yourself. It just shows a severe lack of accountability and responsibility and proves that the person is willing to give up precious things which must be cherished, just to prove their loyalty.

That's the way I loved you

Anderlin

This description of a relationship having partners going back and forth in their decisions reminds me of the song called, "Mannipaaya" by A. R. Rahman. It essentially has the heroine singing out to the hero for forgiveness and that she's sorry for giving him on and off hints of having a relationship. This song has a special place in my heart.

It's in the little things

Anderlin

Receiving handmade gifts are another great example of enjoying the little things you get in life. My sister made me a unique card which had different sections with little descriptions of us having wonderful experiences. Things like these are to die for and I'm genuinely thankful for bein able to receive them.

Losing your best friend

Anderlin

I remember having this experience when my best friend got into a relationship. I was on the phone with him and he just got annoyed by me. That made me rethink my position in his life. It hurts very much when you know you have been replaced but you know you have to be happy for them.

I just grew apart from him to stop bothering him.

Someone to talk to

Anderlin

The part where you said about people being less judgmental when they don't know you very well is actually true. When I meet new people and they share stuff about their lives, I automatically view their lives from a third person perspective and give them an honest opinion so that they can feel a bit at ease when they talk to me. And it's a lot more calming to talk to people this way.

Keeping promises

Anderlin

At the end of the day, it's important to remember that we were the ones to choose whom we should count on. So if they end up breaking that promise, they must've had a pretty good reason as to why they broke it in the first place. That's how you view that from the other person's perspective.

Comfort

Anderlin

That's actually true. I love silence and solitude. I find it relaxing when I'm alone. When the noise of the outside world is tuned out, it helps me to calm my mind. But this can't be true for everyone as others might find that maddening.

Turning off your emotions

Anderlin

Trying to cut off emotions so you are more focused on your goals is the thinking of a fanatic. I'd suggest for you to be more in touch with your emotions because losing your emotions is equivalent of losing yourself.

Who's Afraid Of Little Old Me?

Anderlin

I really wonder what the story of the narrator might be. What pushed her to be seen as a villain among those people. I can relate to villains a lot because I'm seen as a villain in my life as well. And it's so good to hear what the villain's motives are. Remember: Villains are just unspoken heroes.

Girl Code

Anderlin

It's indeed a cruel world. It's good to know that other women look out for each other and got their backs when faced with endangerment. Chivalry might be dead, but women still keep the kindness from their part real.

A Girl's Girl

Anderlin

A supportive woman who cherishes the bonds of other women and validates their success by celebrating their accomplishments? She sounds like one fine woman.

About The Author

Lekhaa MeenakshiSundaram is a young and ambitious writer who published her first book The Werewolves of Brooklyn: Siege of the Dokkalfar as she began her college life. It was always her dream to become a writer. She grew up reading books of various genres which naturally led to her discovering her passion for writing. She has always been a lover of all things supernatural and often finds herself revolving around the world of fantasy and fiction.

She is also an idealist when it comes to womanhood. This motivated her to publish her personal blog *I Just Wanna Be A Girl*, which iterates the trials and tribulations in her personal life. It also throws light on her interests, likes, and dislikes.